FINDERS

Aidan de Vries

FINDERS

Erser & Pond

Published in Canada by Erser & Pond Publishers, Ltd.
1096 Queen St., Suite 225, Halifax, N.S., Canada B3H 2R9

Cover design by Benjamin Beaumont
Cover photo ©iStockphoto.com/gmutlu

Library and Archives Canada Cataloguing in Publication

De Vries, Aidan, author
    Finders / Aidan de Vries.

ISBN 978-0-9865683-8-1 (pbk.)

    I. Title.

PS8607.E97F55 2013   C813'.6   C2013-906193-2

*This book is dedicated to all those who
seek excellence under an equally
excellent governing body.*

"It is a bad plan that admits of no modification."
—Publilius Syrus, Maxim 469,
written in the first century B.C.

CAST OF CHARACTERS

HENRY QUINCE	President of the United States of North America
IVAN WELLAND, PhD	Cabinet Secretary, Dept. of Federal Personnel
COL. CRAIG CUTLER	Chief Officer, Army Helicopter Squadron
BARRY MENDELSON	Special Agent, Internal Revenue Service
BROOKLYN	Assistant to Secretary Ivan Welland
MIKE DICKERSON, J.D.	U.S. Attorney for D.C.
DAMIAN RUTLEDGE, PhD	Finder, Sr. Research Fellow
BYRON BEGLEY, LLB	Finder, ex F.B.I. agent
DAVID FEINGOLD, PhD	Assistant to Secretary Ivan Welland
BRADLEY BURKE	U.S. Chief Negotiator to the U.S.N.A.

MARINA WELLAND, PhD	Wife of Ivan Welland
CDR. MARY O'NEAL	U.S. Naval Officer
CAPTAIN JOHN MERCER	U.S. Navy Seal Officer
LORRAINE PLOUFFE	Secretary of State for the U.S.N.A.
GENE BARKER	Attorney General
CATHERINE WILSON	Nat'l Security Advisor
SERGEI CHERNOVSKY	President of Russia
OLGA YUKOVICH	Russian Agent
IVAN YUKOVICH	Son of Olga and Ivan

CHAPTER ONE

After the unification of Canada and the United States, which everyone had said would be impossible to achieve, the mood of the citizens was one of elation. The formation of the U.S.N.A. (the United States of North America) had been an unparalleled success. Henry Quince, a relatively unknown author and political philosopher, had written a book suggesting that Canada and the United States unite, and it became a best seller as his ideas eventually caught on with the citizens of both countries. People on both sides of the border began to clamor for a formal investigation of the proposition of joining the two nations.

Following the example of the negotiation of NAFTA (the North American Free Trade Agreement), the President of the United States and the Prime Minister of Canada both agreed to appoint a tripartite committee to study the idea and make a recommendation as to whether to hold a plebiscite on the matter. Henry Quince was asked to chair the committee and serve as a neutral party, since he was a dual citizen.

The Americans appointed Bradley Burke, their most experienced and successful international negotiator, to be their representative. The Canadian Prime Minister chose Germain (Gerry) Pelchat, a big player in Canadian financial circles, to be their envoy. With Henry Quince acting as referee, the two heavyweights battled it out. It took a year, but the results were positive and a referendum was decided upon.

The next year, in a hotly contested election, the voters approved the referendum, authorizing the formation of a united North America. After the terms of the incumbent leaders had expired, the ever-popular Henry Quince—a fair-minded individual who had miraculously gained the respect of both the Republicans and the Democrats without formally committing himself to either party—was elected by popular demand to be the first President of The United States of North America. Quince was proud to be the leader of the first major superpower to be dedicated to peaceful, harmonious prosperity.

It became a reality on a scale that even the far-sighted Henry Quince couldn't have predicted. He claimed there was nothing new about his ideas regarding citizenship and good public administration. He used to say, "Government is next to godliness. It must be clean, incorruptible, and selfless."

The election of Henry Quince had been a wake-up call for the two major American political parties, and needless to say, they woke up angry. That a candidate with no political affiliations could beat out either of the establishment choices was anathema to the Washington political inner sanctum. The normal adversarial relationship of the Republican and Democrat parties was scrapped in an effort to show the interloper that he could expect no support from either party.

The old-line politicians were unaffected by the fact that the citizens had clearly shown their displeasure with both of the parties at the polls. The politicians refused, as always, to put the needs and aspirations of the bold new nation before party objectives. The climate of popular unification had gone over the heads of the party leaders. The usual Washington insiders on both sides of the spectrum were busy plotting and calculating how they could make the President's term in office a singularity of living hell.

The views and predictions of the pollsters and pundits had grossly misjudged the voting temper of the American and Canadian people. The influential opinion-makers were discredited by the results at the polls, but instead of getting on board to give the people what they wanted, they surreptitiously rejected the popular majority view in favor of rule by an elite group of political hacks, regardless of the wishes of the electorate.

President Quince had anticipated that the floodgates of Washington bile would be released on him, but even he was surprised by the speed and strength of the opposition coming from both sides of the political spectrum. Their reaction was similar to that of the participants in a domestic dispute when a third party interferes. It was astonishing how organized and cooperative the two adversarial parties could be when they were challenged by an outsider. Being without the help of thousands of party flunkies, fund-raising organizations, and media support, Quince was seen to be weak and vulnerable by the establishment people in the two major parties.

As the forces of opposition lined up against the new President, he used the time between his election and his inauguration to good effect. During his life he had had ample time to meet and assess the capabilities of those around him. He had put forward his platform, the electorate had chosen it, and now he would carry it forward on behalf of his majority constituency no matter what the opposition.

His political opponents had treated his ideas as if they were coming from a simpleton. The leaders of the monotheistic religions accused him of having a Messiah complex, seeking to subvert the holy figures of faith with his own brand of religion that posed as democratic government. His attempts to purge partisan party politics from the governing process were hooted down by those who held public office, for they had much to lose if Quince's programs were to be adopted. But the politicians of the day failed to remember that in a democracy the voters in their constituencies could replace them. They neglected to take into consideration that occasionally the wishes of the masses can prevail over the self-interest of politicians and their political parties.

It had been an enormous surprise when Henry Quince, without party affiliation, had been elected President of the United States of North America. It was just as surprising to his political opponents when he immediately got to work merging Canada and the U.S. With one great policy stroke he created a national entity that changed the lives of North Americans for the better.

By the time the official year of unification rolled around, advancements in social media and computer technology had allowed many government improvements to take hold. It was no longer easy to plow the well-worn corridors of political corruption and cronyism. Leaders, now fewer in number, were expected to put forward new ideas. They were expected to be beyond moral reproach, and if they were not, the new real-time techniques of demonstrated transparency quickly exposed any personal flaws or errors in policy logic.

In his speeches President Quince frequently used sports analogies to stress his points. To improve the functioning of government workers, he created an organization known as the Point Guards, whose purpose was to promote success by teaching the value of team performance over individual achievement. The buddy system, already proven to be highly successful in the military, was expanded into the ranks of government workers. Public service unions were disbanded as wages and benefits were brought into line with those in the private sector. The citizens received better government service, civil servants enjoyed greater job satisfaction, and the negotiating function of the unions was obviated.

These new policies revolutionized what it meant to work for the government. No longer was a civil service job a boring, life-long sinecure that attracted mostly people who valued security above the other advantages of employment. Now a career with the government became the first choice of the majority of job seekers, and why not? Wasn't the government supposed to lead the nation's progress into the future?

Eventually the government employee unions had to admit that obligatory opposition to any policies that tried to change its combative collective bargaining position was simply foolish. When the wages and benefits the government was offering its employees were on a par with those of equivalent workers in the private sector, the spotlight focused on the self-serving unions. Their popularity with the members they claimed to serve declined very quickly. Once the unions were exposed as the political front for the Left, their tactics were reviled and dues-paying union membership dropped off precipitously. When the union members realized that they already had pay and benefits that were equivalent to those of all other workers, their continued union membership became moot. At this point Secretary Welland managed to revamp the U.S. civil service code without massive interference from the deflated public service workers unions.

Stewardship of the Point Guards was centered on a revitalized Civil Service Commission that was raised to Cabinet rank and given cross-departmental authority for human resources in the executive branch of the federal government. President Quince had foreseen that no government could be improved without raising standards and also enhancing the motivation of the workers that made it run. Each department head was to act as a point guard.

After his unexpected election, the Chief Executive got straight to work increasing the effectiveness of his government from top to bottom. He recalled that a certain friend of his, when asked what his favorite job would be, had said he would like to be "God's Personnel Manager." The man had held several cabinet level positions and had always been a truly creative accomplisher, so the President granted him the nearest thing to his wish that was in his presidential power— he named him Secretary of the brand new Department of Federal Personnel, with Cabinet ranking.

This new Secretary was Dr. Ivan Welland. During his term in office the main emphasis of government employment moved from mostly bread-and-butter issues to standards of performance that brooked no lapses into moral turpitude. The Secretary expected and received this level of job performance from his workers because he had instituted a merit system that recognized accomplishments on the part of his employees from the lowest level on up. He thus moved them from the antiquated, compartmentalized seniority structuring instituted by the Civil Service to a refreshingly new system of performance expectation that was complemented by rewards for meritorious functioning. The new standards set up by Secretary Welland required that the number of government employees be reduced. He insisted that the payroll of the U.S. government be reduced substantially, as it had been inflated for far too many years. His philosophy was that by recruiting the most competent people to work for the federal government, fewer would be needed. Therefore hiring the best people for Uncle Sam became the top priority for the new Secretary, who set about turning his thoughts into action without further delay.

Obviously Secretary Welland could not accomplish an entire revitalization of the Civil Service on his own, so he began to recruit his senior staff immediately. During his long tenure in government and private industry he had worked with assistants who had served him well, so he decided to contact some of these to see if any of his proven associates would assist him with the task before he widened his search to include candidates who were unknown to him personally. The sooner he could bring his key people aboard, the sooner he could get on with the assignment President Quince had given him. Advisors who were with him when he had been Secretary of State, Defense, or National Security Advisor were now officially retired, but they continued to function on boards of directors, or as think tank members, or as freelance writers, so it was possible that they could be available and interested in a term assignment as an Under Secretary or as a staffer for Welland as he acted in his new Cabinet position. With this in mind the Secretary began a telephone campaign to reenlist his preferred co-workers in a new and worthy cause. He began by calling his long-time friend, adjutant, and amanuensis, Dr. David Feingold.

"David, it's Ivan. How are you?"

"I'm fine thanks, and yourself?"

"Great physically, but I'm guessing you've heard that I've gotten myself in a spot of trouble with another of those quirky assignments that I seem to be prone to. Naturally I'm wondering if you'd be willing to help bail me out again."

"I was wondering when you were going to call."

"I'm trying to put the old gang back in operation. Would you like to serve as my second in command once again?"

"I'm still at the think tank, Ivan, but I can get a leave of absence if one is required. You realize I don't know a thing about the Civil Service, though, except that I've been on the payroll a couple of times in the past."

"That'll do just fine. The last thing I want to do, David, is help perpetuate the situation for the two million employees of the federal government. So may I count on your help?"

"Of course. What do you want me to do?"

"Just bring whatever projects you're working on now to a close. We'll have our first planning session in two weeks. I'll call you soon to let you know the time and place of the meeting, and who I've been able to recruit to serve with us."

"Sounds good. I'll expect your call then. Good luck with your recruiting. I bet I'll see some familiar faces."

"You will, David. Thanks for coming aboard."

Ivan continued down his call list. When he asked people to jump, their usual reaction was to ask how high. At a height of six foot seven, when Ivan Welland put his massive hand on a shoulder, people acquiesced. His graying black hair and steely blue eyes served to inspire cooperation rather than obedience. Secretary Welland was a true leader, full of confidence but always patient and eager to hear an opposing view. Those who had worked with him before would always be ready to serve.

Just as Ivan Welland had known exactly who he would ask to help him, so President Quince had mentally selected those he wanted to have close to him during his administration. Since Henry Quince was independent of party affiliations, he had the advantage of choosing his compatriots without the interference and prejudice of others, however well-meaning the advisors might be. He owed nobody any favors, so his choices were based solely on his judgment of the character and abilities of his candidates for each position. This resulted in the appointment of a cabinet composed of people who were not always well known on the national political scene. Because Quince had lived in Canada for half his life, he was able to call on a number of able Canadians to accept leadership positions within the newly amalgamated nation. These nominees were unknown to most Americans, and their anonymity to U.S. journalists and cynical old-line politicos would help squelch the media, at least for the beginning of the Quince administration. Ivan Welland was perhaps the best known of Quince's American appointees. His name was recognized by most of the members of the newly constituted Senate when it was sent over for confirmation.

Ivan Welland respected the new President. He knew that it was courageous of him to put forward his candidacy as an independent. In Ivan's opinion, Quince had not done it for egotistical reasons. He was determined to help the President implement the policies in his platform, which was an ambitious one and one of which Ivan greatly approved. He shared Henry Quince's disappointment over the way the office of the President of the United States had previously fallen into the hands of party hacks of one kind or another, and he was determined to bring about major changes in the way the government of the U.S.N.A. would be managed.

When Quince had completed the slate of appointees that he intended to send to the Senate, he invited everyone on his list to a meeting at which they could get acquainted with those who soon would be their colleagues. At this preview cabinet meeting Quince delivered an address in which he detailed all the things he intended to do during his first term. He invited those present to submit ideas for administering the area of government to which they had been appointed.

He promised to read all their plans and proposals before they were sworn in, and to return them with his suggestions or comments and hopefully with his approval. He expected to have the basic direction of each department in his Executive Branch settled so the work could be started at the first real cabinet meeting to be held the day after his inauguration. By the time the group photo of the incoming new cabinet was taken, the Secretaries and senior staff were all acquainted, clear about their individual and collective tasks, and ready to go to work.

Likewise in Ivan Welland's new Department of Federal Personnel, the departmental mission statement, the flow chart of the newly divided areas of responsibility, and the pertinent staffing and budgeted operating costs of each segment of the DFP were established before the start of business on Inauguration Day. This had not been an easy task, for it included the amalgamation of all the government functions of both Canada and the U.S., which formed a big part of the assimilation of the two nations into the United States of North America. Nine years had passed after the publication of Quince's little book that proposed that a bi-lateral committee be struck to consider whether a referendum should be held, what it should ask, and if approved, whether the merger of the two nations should be binding. Once the referendum passed, the most important feature of every government department on either side of the border was to anticipate and smooth out every kink in the management of the merger. Bradley Burke, the chief U.S. merger negotiator and Ivan's friend and colleague from their days at the non-profit Foundation for Democracy Research, was put in charge of merger details by the President on Ivan's recom-mendation. President Quince himself, who up until that time had been a relatively unknown author and political philoso-pher, now became the CEO of North America.

Ivan's challenge during the course of the merger was to blend the civil services of Canada and the U.S. into one efficiently functioning government. He appointed David Feingold to be his Chief of Staff and "Brooklyn" Brocklyn, his former secretary and talented administrative assistant, to be his Deputy Project Manager. Damian Rutledge, the "old man" of the team, was assigned to blend the departmental operation manuals into one publication that would serve as the new rulebook for merged employees from both countries. Dr. Welland maintained the executive role of civil service overlord, and he also retained the operations leadership of a special small internal group that he created and nicknamed *The Finders*. This semi-secret elite group was charged with the responsibility for recruiting senior people with special skills that were needed by the various departments of the U.S.N.A. The Finders were President Quince's headhunters. They would locate and persuade the most capable people in the world to come to the newly united countries and take up citizenship in the U.S.N.A. to enjoy the numerous career opportunities that the merger was creating.

In President Quince's campaign for election he spoke out strongly against the former immigration policies of the United States, which in his opinion had been far too liberal, too politically correct, too largely based on family nepotism, and lacking cohesion. It was his idea to halt all immigration to the U.S.N.A. until the immigration regulations could be rewritten, redirected, and tightened up. He was not at all against immigration or immigrants *per se*—quite the opposite in fact. Ivan Welland, following Quince's lead, wanted the U.S.N.A.'s new immigration policies to be designed to enhance the knowledge bank of the nation's citizenry, and this is where The Finders came in. This influential group of recruiters would scour the world to find individuals of the highest caliber to contribute their talents to critical areas of government, science, and academia, and then persuade them to immigrate to the U.S.N.A.

CHAPTER TWO

E nvy, perhaps the ugliest of the seven deadly sins, was at the root of the hatred that the professional politicians in Washington had for President Henry Quince. Perhaps because envy is loaded with selfishness and ego, it exploded in the faces of the greedy power brokers in the new nation's capital. The deals that had been the stock in trade of the political cognoscenti in Washington were halted like a train running head-on into another oncoming train. Pieces of the wreck were everywhere to be found. Deals made had to be withdrawn, deals in the making had to be cancelled, and deals contemplated had to be abandoned. Those who had been involved in surreptitiously dividing up the government pork pie had to be relieved of that privilege, no matter how unpleasant that might be for them. If President Quince could get himself elected in spite of the enmity that ran rampant in the capital, then he very well might be able to live up to his promise to clean up Washington. When Quince overturned the apple cart belonging to the bipartisan politicos by getting elected, he not only revealed the worms in the apples, but he also maddened the vipers camped beneath the apple cart.

Henry Quince was an idealist, but he was nobody's fool. He realized that he was going to disturb a lot of important people by implementing the changes he had promised during the campaign. Many of them would be the deadly overseas partners of the domestic rats at home. Even Quince could not have imagined the magnitude of fury he could generate by merely mentioning the word "change". Some years before, President Obama had discovered for himself that change was easy to promise, but nearly impossible to effect. Quince, however, unlike his predecessors, wasn't willing to take the easy road and let his promised changes slide slowly into the malignant mire that was the status quo. Quince wondered why the past presidents of the United States and the prime ministers of Canada had never had the wisdom and courage to follow the admonition that George Washington had made in his farewell address when he warned his successors about the deleterious effects of political parties on democracy.

An honest man, pledged to keeping his promises to the people of North America, was just what was needed to bring the merger of the United States and Canada to a successful conclusion. Out there in the world, however, were powerful forces that saw the merger as a way of providing hegemony to the West, and they couldn't abide it. Many of the nations of the world practiced assassination as the preferred way to remove unwanted leaders, and nobody knew this better than Ivan Welland. His prior experiences in matters of homeland security had left no doubts in his mind that President Quince had made himself a target for those who hated American style democracy and for those who violently opposed the formation of a united and more powerful North America. Ivan was pledged to serve and protect the man who had put his life on the line to promote "freedom through strength" on the Continent. He wrestled with the seeming contradiction of his new position as Secretary of Federal Personnel and the responsibility for protecting the President. He finally solved his jurisdictional dilemma by remembering that as head of the civil service he was responsible for the selection of government employees, including those charged with protecting the President.

As Ivan Welland took up his new duties, he decided to set up meetings with a number of very important government department heads so that they could discuss his concerns and attempt to set up some anticipatory steps in advance of any crises that might arise. To facilitate these meetings he made personal calls to every senior government official who might have on his list of duties anything relating to the protection of the President. Ivan noticed a distinct difference in attitude on the part of this President's appointees. In the past they would have had territorial rivalries and personality conflicts galore about crossing departmental borderlines. But here there was no trace of the turf wars that might have been anticipated in the past. Ivan attributed the new attitude to the personality of the President. Henry Quince was a good man, but there was a no-nonsense element about him that made his would-be opponents reluctant to go to the mat with him. The President had spine and owed no one any favors. He was not like those handshaking grandstanders who fought their way to the top through the morass of party politics that forced them to remain connected to their supporters by obligations and debts.

Dr. Welland was very pleased with what he had seen of Quince in office so far. At their next private meeting he took up the issue of the President's personal vulnerability, and put in a positive word about the spirit of cooperation that he had encountered in Quince's other appointees. He also informed the President of his intention to use the Finders group as a covert cadre of elite headhunters. He told Quince that if there were a skill the nation needed, or an individual whose contributions could be significant, or someone the President would like to meet quietly behind closed doors, the Finders would make the arrangements. Ivan also pointed out to Quince that no one but the two of them would know that the members of the Finders would each have taken Navy Seal training and could be counted on for 100% loyalty to him alone in the event of any crisis.

In his peculiar way Secretary Ivan Welland had been preparing for his present job all his life. He kept a little black book that had nothing to do with his social life but everything to do with the life of his country. In this book he jotted down the names and personal information of all the people he had met over the years who might be good candidates for membership in the Finders. Now at last he would have need of that special list as he formed his dream team.

Ivan knew he was entering unknown territory, exceeding by a mile the previous authority level of the person in charge of the Civil Service, but ultimately the man responsible for hiring and firing was the President. Even so, no individual could supervise two million government employees without a lot of help. Ivan saw his job as being the right-hand man to the President when dealing with human resource matters. Fortunately, the President saw it that way too. Ivan's next job was to recruit those keepers who would be his Finders.

He delved into his little black book and came up with the names of two junior naval officers—one male and one female—who had worked with him many years before when they had stymied a terrorist attack on a huge, newly launched cruise ship. In this conflict the two naval officers had served with fearless distinction, saving the lives of many innocent people. By now they might be staff officers, or they could be disinterested in the assignment he had in mind for them. Perhaps they were no longer in the military, but he would check on their current status and find out.

He also had in mind a young helicopter pilot who had flown him in and out of trouble in Saudi Arabia, and later piloted him on several adventures during the years of his career in government service. In a different sort of venue he had recorded in his black book the name of a young assistant U.S. attorney who once had performed a legal miracle right in the face of his crooked boss, the Attorney General.

He remembered his assistant Brooklyn's husband, Barry Mendelson, an Internal Revenue special agent who had later fathered his favorite godson. He also recalled Byron Begley, the F.B.I. agent who helped to put an end to an election fraud of immense importance to the nation's democratic processes, losing his fiancée who had died during the affair. These were some of the people who would not make it into the Guinness Book of Records, but who did make it into Ivan's personal record book. These people would now have to be contacted and reviewed for their suitability as Finders. All in all, Ivan felt his old black book would serve him well to seed his new crew of "Black Ops" civil servant recruiters.

Ivan Welland, the Secretary of Federal Personnel, had made it known to his senior colleagues in the various cabinet departments that his Finders stood ready to do sensitive, urgent recruitment jobs that lay outside the normal operations of the previous Civil Service directors.

Ivan had made it perfectly clear that his function would be a proactive one. He didn't intend to sit back and wait for job applicants to happen along—he was going to go out and find the best people to do those special jobs. For decades the Civil Service had been doing all the functions of a corporate personnel department. They administered exams, posted job openings, wrote manuals, trained staff, handled employment details such as salary matters, explained benefits, calculated pensions, doled out promotions, and handled the enormous number of details involved in managing the employees of the Federal Government. The function they failed to do was perhaps the most important one of all: they did not aggressively recruit to find the best or most unusual candidates to fill the available openings.

Ivan meant to change that. He was not going to be the head of the Civil Service without being the head headhunter. He was certain that attention to that neglected function was going to make all the difference between his administration of the Civil Service and that of his predecessors. He had discussed these matters with the President and had obtained his unqualified support. Ivan believed that the one department which sorely needed his services was the former INS. The Immigration and Naturalization Service, because of 9/11 and the drug-running problem, had essentially surrendered its original purpose and was now more concerned with homeland security problems than with immigration matters. As a result the functioning of the INS was now directed more at keeping the wrong people out of the United States than it was in admitting the *right* people into the country.

Throughout its history the INS had been bounced around the halls of government. At various different times it had reported to the Attorney General, The Department of Labor, The Department of Commerce, and lately to the Department of Homeland Security. This orphan agency of the federal government had bravely tried to conduct its ever-changing business, but like a kicked-off football on a windy, rainy day it had erratically ricocheted from governmental pillar to post, always changing its intended direction and its thrust. It was time for the function to be rescued, its purpose clarified, and its energy focused. Ivan Welland was just the person to see to it, but for the moment it was not in his purview.

That would have to change.

Getting something new done in Washington was like being in a room that had been occupied by many spiders. On the one hand, to a casual observer their webs seemed to be connected, but each spinner knew and guarded his own web. It was not in the nature of a bureaucratic Washington spider to give way or cooperate in any scheme that would reduce the span of his particular web.

Ivan knew this from his years in government service, but he had often overcome that attitude on the part of the incumbent spiders of the past by having a clear mandate from the chief spider himself. President Quince knew that too, and he had reminded Ivan that he had been elected to bring about change and efficiencies in the government, not to pussy foot around internal departmental territorial disputes. He expected Ivan Welland, with his full presidential authorization, to be the Secretary of Federal Personnel and to do whatever he felt was necessary to streamline the flowchart of the Executive Branch of the federal government, while protecting the citizens of the new country according to the basic intentions of the Constitution of the U.S.N.A. As presently constituted the function of admitting people to residency and then eventual citizenship was delegated to the merged U.S. Citizenship & Immigration Service and the Canadian equivalent. Matters such as permanent residency, naturalization and asylum became the responsibility of the USCIS. The investigative and enforcement functions, including all deportations and intelligence, had originally been the responsibility of the U.S. Immigration and Customs Enforcement (ICE), but now the North American border protection functions had been combined. U.S. and Canadian Customs Inspectors were now called U.S.N.A. Customs and Border Protection (CBP).

The parent agency for all of these agencies became the unified Department of Justice. At first the legal admission of immigrants continued to be passive, functioning with rules, of course, but very politically correct ones. At this point no effort was being expended to have a proactive immigration policy. Immigrant applications were received without regard to color, race, religion, or nation of origin, which was fine, but it resulted in the merged USCIS and the Canadian Immigration Service being overwhelmed with applications from people wanting to come to the U.S.N.A., the majority of whom the citizens of the U.S.N.A. didn't wish to admit.

Welland would have to speak to the Attorney General about correcting this matter. Ivan suspected that the laws and regulations relating to immigration traced back to the 19th century when open land was still available and immigrants were needed to fill it. In the 21st century, however, the need for immigrants was a vastly different one. Population growth over the centuries had reduced the need for laborers to work on farms and in industry. Now, technological advancements required immigrants with top levels of education and of the highest moral character. The U.S.N.A. was not looking for people who simply wanted to come to North America—it sought those whom it wished to invite. As far as Ivan was concerned, being someone's relative was no longer sufficient to qualify would-be immigrants for automatic entrance to North America.

Ivan hoped that Attorney General Gene Barker would feel the same way as he did about tightening up the standards for admission to U.S. citizenship. He wanted Barker to agree to keep a large number of permanent residencies open for his Finders, so that if they located an applicant of rare abilities they could process the candidate through the paperwork in a short time. He wanted his relationship with the Attorney General to be one of trust and cooperation. With this in mind he had asked Brooklyn to connect him right away to the government's chief lawyer, a man he had met at the one brief meeting with the President's cabinet, and whose legal credentials were known to be sterling.

"Gene, this is Ivan Welland. I have an important matter I'd like to discuss with you off the record."

"Okay Ivan, what is it?"

"I don't know if you've heard that I want to set up an elite recruiting function that I've named the Finders. We're going to use it pro-actively to solicit immigrants who possess extraordinary abilities that the U.S.N.A. can readily employ to our advantage. There may be some occasions in the course of this recruiting when we'll need an expedited Permanent Resident visa to get someone through the immigration red tape in a hurry. I need to know that if and when such a case arises, I can depend upon your department to cooperate fully. Naturally we'll reciprocate by keeping your department in the picture as much as possible. If you wish, we could keep this just between us, or if you'd rather, we can set up some sort of departmental fast-track procedure. What do you say?"

"I've heard the President speak of this idea, and I agree that it's an excellent one. We want to have a procedure that can sidestep the red tape in those cases when efficiency and speed can make the difference. So I would definitely like to cooperate in every way I can. If we keep this between us we should be able to ram the odd visa through on short notice, I should think."

"That suits me just fine," Ivan said, feeling relieved and encouraged by the Attorney General's attitude. "Thanks for your understanding, Gene. We're just getting this effort in motion, so it may be a while before you hear from me again on this matter."

"I can see where you're coming from on this one. Why shouldn't we cherry-pick occasionally? God knows we let a million people in with few or no credentials. Why shouldn't we pick and choose some of the more important ones from time to time?"

"You got it," Ivan said, smiling.

"So thanks for the courtesy call, Ivan. I'll look forward to hearing from you again."

In the capitals of Europe, hostility towards the newly merged nation in North America was building. At the root of the enmity was the shame concerning how the European Union had failed to produce either unity or prosperity for the multinational populations that comprised the organization, while the merger of the North American giants seemed to be progressing well. Europeans had always been suspicious of one another, and considering the enormity of the task of putting centuries of war and hatred aside, the European Union had enjoyed considerable success. The problem in Europe was impatience and unrealistic expectations. The countries whose national personality traits included passion and spontaneity were unwilling or unable to wait patiently while they built the economic infrastructure that would support prosperity on a pan-European level.

On the other hand, the leading economically developed European countries were loath to help or share their good fortune with their poorer neighbors, especially when they were acting like entitled spoiled children unwilling to take responsibility for their own debts. While Europe flitted about from problem to problem, the U.S.N.A. was beginning the largest boom cycle the world had ever seen. Like crabs in a fisherman's basket, the Europeans pulled one another down, not realizing that their real enemy was the fisherman. Had they cooperated, they could easily have escaped from the basket.

A larger problem for the U.S.N.A. was the enmity of the Russians. The leaders of Russia had never quite gotten over the losses caused by the break-up of the Soviet Union. That Union had been held together by force of compulsion. When the poorly run Communist regime could no longer afford to compete with the successful Western nations, their satellite nations deserted to freedom in a flash. This was bound to happen. After all, when a boot is removed from his throat, the prisoner escapes as quickly as possible. However, what remained of Russia was still the largest nation on earth, but it lacked wealth and power when compared with the democracies of the West. What it did have underpinning its future was a treasure-trove of minerals and fossil fuels. Drawing on this wealth, particularly its oil reserves, to produce a competitive modern economy in a hurry, the Russian leaders were strutting around as if their good fortune had been due to good management.

In truth, what was going on in Russia was a power grab by gangsters of the old school who were still trying to make corruption the principal vehicle of success, as they had done with Soviet style communism. The leaders of modern Russia hated the example that Quince's U.S.N.A. provided to the people of the world. The very survival of the current leaders of Russia could, in fact, depend on their making certain that President Quince and the U.S.N.A. suffered an enormous, embarrassing failure.

Catherine Wilson, the President's National Security Advisor, was holding forth on this subject at the first full meeting of President Quince's Cabinet.

"Mr. President," she declared, "you can't think for a moment that your life is secure. There are people in this world who wouldn't hesitate for a second to assassinate you if they thought they could, and the sooner the better. That's how a good many nations would like to deal with a problem like you."

"Now Catherine, don't exaggerate."

"Mr. President, it's not a bit of an exaggeration. No one wants to appear to be inept. In comparison to the European leaders, with the exception of the U.K. and Germany, what you've done in North America puts them all to shame. But the worst is Russia. Chernovsky stays in power by greasing the palms of his Russian mafia supporters who, ever since the dissolution of the USSR, are enriching themselves as a result of the privatization of the petroleum reserves in the Caspian Basin. What's going on in Russia is the biggest separation between the wealthy and the poor in the whole history of the world. Right now there are more millionaires in Moscow than in any other city in the world. If the extent of this gets back to the hoi polloi in Russia—and it must eventually, what with all the many forms of electronic media out there in the world—Chernovsky and his gang of thieves will be doomed. But if they can keep their deals quiet, or if they can shift the blame to the U.S.N.A. or, in other words, make *you* responsible, then they can look like heroes to the Russian people for making things a little better than they were under Communism. They were the largest country in the world until you came along and created the U.S.N.A. So the loss of superpower status, if it were to be publicized in Russia, would not redound to the benefit of Chernovsky and his boys. Their success is the result of becoming a big fish in a much smaller pond."

"That's still a long way from assassinating me."

"Beware the Ides of March, Mr. President."

"Okay, Catherine, I realize I've got skin in the game. I'll stay on top of Homeland Security to keep me alive, if only so everyone who hates me can have a convenient target to focus their hatred on. But right now I'd like to discuss something our colleague Ivan Welland has suggested. I'm going to call on him now to explain his Finders group. Ivan."

"Thank you Mr. President," Ivan said, standing up and addressing the Cabinet. "I think all of you will agree that our Administration is only as good as the people in it. It's the same with the country itself—we're only as good as the citizens. Since the 1891 Immigration Act made immigration a federal responsibility in the U.S., we've kicked the quality can down the road. At first, immigration laws were made by the States to serve their needs for laborers. Citizenship was not much of a concern until after the Civil War. Freed slaves automatically became citizens, who then became voters. The industrial North needed workers for its factories, the bread-basket States needed farmers, and people in Europe were offered land if they'd come and work it. After a while the nation was flooded with people from poor countries who wanted to become Americans. When we decided to staunch the flow people we imposed quotas on Europeans based on the number of immigrants from the countries that were already represented here in the U.S. Then on humanitarian grounds we gave preference to the relatives of those immigrants who had already been admitted."

Ivan paused to take a sip of water.

"Occasionally, when shortages of certain skilled workers arose," he went on, "we gave preference to those immigrants with needed skills. We compliment ourselves on opening our borders to people needing asylum. So as you can see, our immigration policies have been all over the place. But ever since 9/11 we've had to increase background checks and various other security measures in regard to immigration and naturalization. Nowadays we attempt to delve as deeply as possible into the past histories of the people we admit as potential citizens. Over the years the service rendered by the Immigration and Naturalization Service has moved around the Cabinet table almost as much as I have, changing its reporting from one executive branch to another, from Labor, to Commerce, to Treasury, to Homeland Security, and to the Justice Department, where it resides now. The world has changed a good bit since mass immigration to the United States and Canada became popular. The point is, we need a purposefully directed national program for immigration, and we need it right now."

There was a rumble of mutterings around the room, and Welland put up his hand for silence.

"I would like to propose that we begin to work on one immediately," he continued. "Until the policy is ready to put in place, I'd like us to suspend immigration, on a temporary basis, until we've had a chance to prepare a new immigration policy for the 21st century. I'm also suggesting that we get the Finders up and running as soon as possible. We need to stop waiting for remarkable immigrants to come to us. We need to create a specific method whereby we can reach out to the ones *we* want in our country. The best educated, most desirable candidates for citizenship may not be lined up to come here anymore. You may remember that after V-E day, when we wanted to get German rocket technology before the Russians got hold of it, we spirited Werner Von Braun out of Germany and brought him to America, where we put him in charge of our rocketry program. That one piece of head-hunting, along with preventive kidnapping, permitted us to beat the Russians to the moon. So what I'm looking for now is an elite corps of headhunter recruiters on standby and available to any and all cabinet secretaries, military chiefs, and senior scientists who want a particular person to help speed up progress with important projects in the U.S.N.A."

Ivan paused to take a sip of water, then he nodded at a woman in the front row who had raised her hand.

"Welland, are you suggesting that we cruise around the world picking off the top people in any important field we choose, and then spirit them off to the U.S.N.A.?"

The question came from the Secretary of State, Lorraine Plouffe, and the former Canadian Minister of Foreign Affairs whom Quince had nominated because she carried an air of Canadian neutrality about her that he hoped would tone down any assumption of American belligerence that envious nations might develop.

The chuckles around the table subsided as the very tall Secretary of Federal Personnel gravely replied.

"I think we should make them an offer they can't refuse. After all, any International Corporation searching for a CEO would think nothing of hiring an executive search firm to test the employment waters with any candidate they coveted to do their job. I really don't see how, in a competitive world like ours, this could be out of line. I'm not advocating that we kidnap people, of course, and the candidates can always just say no."

At the end of a short open discussion, the Cabinet decided that Welland should go ahead with his Finders corps as long as he didn't create any international incidents.

CHAPTER THREE

L ater that day the secure phone rang in Secretary Ivan Welland's office. When he picked it up he heard the familiar voice of his colleague, Catherine Wilson, the National Security Advisor.

"Hello, Catherine. What can I do for you?"

"You can jolly well care more about your future."

"What are you talking about?"

"I'm talking about the precautions, or should I say, lack of precautions you're taking."

"Why? What have I done now?"

"I see you're planning to waltz around the planet with your Finders without the benefit of security forces. You are a Cabinet level official of the United States. We can't have you or the members of your staff getting knocked off by the first assassin who comes along. That would be bad publicity for the country and even worse publicity for you. It wouldn't be too good for your staff, either."

"But our headhunting must be done in secret, Catherine. If we arrive en masse we may tip our hand that we're trying to hire one of their stars away, or perhaps kidnap one."

"So send someone else. Someone with a lower profile. You can provide your surrogate with a letter of authorization from you. You needn't be present in person, Ivan."

"You think it's a question of my ego getting involved?"

"Yes. I do."

"Well maybe it is, and that's not right. Okay then, I'll work out the arrangements with you and the Secretary of Homeland Security before I go traipsing off, and if I can, I'll send a lieutenant in my place. How does that suit you?"

Ivan quickly thought about Catherine's position and had decided that the National Security Advisor was correct. His getting bumped off would be bad news for the President, and it might also signify to terrorists that it was open season on officials of the U.S.N.A.

Catherine Wilson was taken aback by Welland's sudden tractability. She had not counted on his ability to see both sides of the argument. Ivan, for his part, realized that she was trying to do her job, and he liked her feistiness in sticking to her guns when she thought she was right. The incident was only a small one, but it was indicative of the new Cabinet's desire to work together under their new leader. The newly elected government was going to work better now than the previous ones because the internal turf war borders stopped at the point where the U.S.N.A. national unity issues began.

Ivan was basking in the new era of collegiality when Brooklyn walked into his office with a worried expression on her face. He had seen that look many times before, and he knew what to expect.

"Boss, we're beginning to get requests from several different departments for access to our headhunting services. Colonel Cutler has sent you a wish list of the names of people that come from every corner of our new government. You might have promised more than we can deliver. Take a look at the list of Russians that our people would like to send over here, for example. I've tried to gather a short dossier of the backgrounds of each of the people on the list."

Ivan took Cutler's list from Brooklyn and began to scan it. Once again his speed-reading skills came to the fore and he quickly deduced that the targeted immigration that he espoused was devoted primarily to people with technical skills—engineers, astrophysicists, nuclear experts, software designers, and the like. One name, however, stuck out from the rest: Olga Yukovich, software designer. He wondered if he should be up front with Cutler and mention to him that he had known her at Princeton, but he had not been favorably impressed with her character. After thinking about it for a bit, Ivan decided that he would give her the benefit of the doubt. She had probably grown up by this time and had her unpleasantly competitive spirit more under control, but could she be trusted if she were to be granted citizenship in the newly formed United States of North America?

Seeing Olga's name on Colonel Cutler's list brought back a flood of other memories which Ivan received with mixed emotions. One of the few good things about Russian Communism was that it freed women to compete with men for careers, wages and status. Lenin's Marxist policies had made it possible for women to rise to the top in certain fields such as medicine, for instance, where 70% of the physicians in Russia were women. Some historians claimed that the equality of the sexes had nothing to do with Communist party liberality. They attributed it to the fact that women had to do these things because of the scarcity of men created by the heavy losses the Russians had sustained in World War II. Russian women also made enormous strides in other fields of endeavor, such as engineering and science.

One area of intellectual attainment in which they did not do very well was in the game of chess. In fact, no woman had ever reached the top ranks of chess players in the world. The title of Grand Master had eluded them, and many fathers of Russian girls wondered why. It seemed that no matter how hard they tried, they always fell short of the top ranks. Marina Welland, Ivan's wife, had been one of these women. Her father had coached her for many years, but although she became a very good chess player she never made it to the rank of Master. Another Russian woman with a similar story was Olga Yukovich, who became a first class computer software designer, but remained a lower-ranked chess player.

Unlike Marina, who had made peace with her inability to become a top chess player, Olga seemed unable to quiet her fierce competitive streak. Her father had been a high officer in the secret police (NKVD) of the Soviet Union, and he had been disappointed by his daughter's chess-playing performance. When she was younger, Olga had been on the

Russian National Volley Ball Team and had won a scholarship to do an advanced degree in math at Princeton, where she converted her math background into a career in computer programming. These were not inconsequential accomplishments, but she always felt that she had let her father down because she failed to reach the master's level in chess tournament play. Her father had belittled her chess playing because she lacked the killer instinct during the end game. Recently, however, she had gained his grudging approval for a skill neither of them had suspected she would have.

It was a peculiar quirk of fate that made Ivan Welland think of Olga again. In previous years he had been a graduate student in the Department of Mathematics at Princeton. Olga had coincidentally also been a foreign student in the same math program. They had been thrown together because they shared several points of interest, talent, and ethnicity. Ivan's Russian grandmother, with whom he was very close, had taken the time to teach him the language as a boy. When it became common knowledge around the Math Department that Ivan spoke Russian, it was assumed that he and Olga would get along well. She was surprised when Welland had spoken to her in Russian, for she thought it unusual for such a young American guy to speak Russian competently. She had laughed at him and told him he spoke like an old woman from the past, but secretly she was impressed.

Chess was a very popular sport among the math nerds at Princeton, but Ivan hadn't played much chess before he arrived there. He had never really studied the game seriously, and never played with anyone who had. He was aware that there was a chess culture with a definite hierarchy, but he had never participated in a tournament. Chess for Welland was a mere diversion. His ego was not involved. He noticed that some of his opponents took it pretty seriously, and these young men got angry—some nearly wept—when he beat them. He thought it foolish to allow a silly game to bruise one's ego. At that time he was totally unaware of the effect that chess and Olga would have on his future life. He didn't think much about it when Olga invited him to play chess with her, and it didn't bother him much that she beat him quite easily. But many times he would recall the episode in his life in which Olga had played such a big part. She was serious about chess, and she took pleasure in annihilating her opponents. Ivan had no idea how devastated Olga would be if he were able to win a chess match against her. Thinking she would enjoy the opportunity of playing with a reasonably competent adversary, he went on a crash program to upgrade his chess-playing skills. He never suspected the demeaning effect it would have on Olga if he succeeded in beating her.

Welland did not have a lot of experience with girls at the time of their meeting. His interests from early childhood had been so cerebral that his hormones never really gained the upper hand. He knew the biology, but his knowledge was basically theoretical and had a laboratory quality about it. Some girls had tried out their wiles on him, but his head was so far in the clouds that he barely knew what he was doing. Until his arrival in New Jersey, he had always lived at home with his parents. Ivan was a prodigy, and at nineteen he was the youngest person in the Masters program at Princeton. He was secretly pleased to have missed all the college sex, alcohol, drugs, and sports. To tell the truth, what little he did know about girls bored him.

But Olga was different. She was twenty-four years old, and more mature than girls of his age. She was self-confident and functioning in a foreign country on her own. She had beaten him at chess, so she had to be smart. She was over six feet tall, and he liked that, as he was six feet seven. He had always felt awkward with girls of average size. There was something that made him uncomfortable about looking down on them. Although he understood Gulliver, he did not understand Olga. She had a head of blond, wiry hair with red tints that made her hair appear slightly pink when the light hit it. Her face was interesting but not exactly beautiful, because her features were blunted, which gave her a bit of a pug nose and the flat, broad face of a peasant. She looked serious and formidable when she concentrated on the chessboard, and Ivan was not attracted to her.

Olga had enjoyed a much more normal teenage life than Ivan. She was a very good student too, but she was also well rounded. She had played volleyball at school and had just missed out on being selected to play for the Russian Olympic team. She had a quick, almost bouncy walk, and had had her share of encounters with the opposite sex. She was unimpressed for the most part by how needy and stupid the men her age were. Being around volleyball players had enabled her to become comfortable with tall people, as all the players in that sport were tall. As a result she was in no way intimidated by Ivan Welland. She could tell right away that he was sweet and inexperienced, but she didn't know whether he was worth bothering about. Her plan was to get her Master's degree, then return to Russia to teach math or become a computer programmer, and possibly coach volleyball on the side. This big little boy was certainly not likely to figure in her future, so why waste time with him?

From his nearly innocent standpoint, Ivan had been oblivious to Olga's sex appeal. His total vagary had always been his strength in dealing with the opposite sex, but he, of course, was unaware of it. The girls were kept off balance by his kindly nature and his interest in almost everything. They never knew if he was being kind to them in particular, or if he was that way with everyone.

Ivan avoided Olga for a few weeks while he studied every book available about chess. He played computer chess in all his spare moments. He studied the famous great games played by grand masters over the last fifty years. His fine memory was a fearsome thing when he applied it to a task. After some time he felt he was ready to play Olga again. He began looking around to find her, but he was careful to make the meeting look like a coincidence. One day, after about five weeks had passed, there she was in the library stacks. He sidled over to her and greeted her in Russian. She looked up, and when she recognized him, she asked after his Babushka. He sensed that she was subtly making fun again of his way of speaking. He loved his grandmother and felt embarrassed for her sake, but he let it go, preferring to get this impertinent Russian girl into a chess game. He asked Olga if she had time for a rematch, and soon they went off together in search of a chessboard.

This time Olga was the one who was surprised. Ivan's game was much stronger than the first time they had played together. She had to use every bit of her skill and experience to eke out a draw. How had this boy managed to improve so much? Had he been asleep during their first match? She felt he would have won this latest match if he had played the white pieces. Luckily for her she had played white, and the advantage of the first move had enabled her to mount a very strong attack, which she had sustained during Ivan's counter-attack, allowing her to end up with a draw. Perhaps there was more to this gentle giant than she had originally thought. She shook her curly head and silently vowed to win their next match.

Ivan, for his part, questioned the place of chess in the hierarchy of games. Certainly it required a high degree of intelligence in order for a player to succeed, but the ratio of draws to clear-cut victories struck Ivan as peculiar. How can a game, which so often ends in a dull tie, earn enough favor to become the national game of Russia? How could so many people stubbornly be satisfied with something so boring? A chess game that results in a victory for one of the players is still only a game that proceeds, with the usual constraints of agreed-upon rules, to signify the mental ascendancy of the victor. In reality, nothing earth-shattering occurs. The victory in itself can be a disappointment because it is temporary, and its tenure extends only until the next game, when the result could just as easily be reversed. If one side consistently wins there is no competition, and consequently there is no sense in playing at all. If one person, by virtue of being intelligent, can always win at chess, the victory is hollow and cruel, something like a master beating a slave. What good can come of that? As to chess being a game that teaches strategy in the military sense, there are many other realistic games that simulate the war situation to a less limiting degree than chess. The element of mental unhealthiness in seeking dominance over another person disturbed Ivan. Worse, it made him question the moral base of the Russian society that gave such importance to this game, and especially so since this was the heritage present in his own genes.

Perhaps, in a vastly expanded way, it was this widely held state of mind that accounted for the long held vision of Russian communism conquering the world. Ivan Welland resolved to beat Olga at chess to demonstrate that American democracy was a better preparation for a meaningful life than the stultifying rules of chess-inspired Russian politics. It would also serve as his bill of divorcement from this ethnic national sport. He resolved to give up chess once he accomplished his mission of repelling Olga's attempt to dominate him, because he felt chess was demeaning for both winner and loser. He felt the motivations for playing chess were ugly, and the acquisition of masterly skills were time wasted.

Ivan's day-dreaming was interrupted when he heard Brooklyn's voice on the intercom, reminding him that he had a meeting scheduled with Catherine Wilson to discuss the security aspects of the Finders' first recruiting assignments.

CHAPTER FOUR

Ivan's recruits had found it quite impossible to refuse the Secretary's job offers. Somehow they all knew that if it was an assignment to a department headed by Dr. Ivan Welland, it was bound to be interesting and different. So when Ivan called them to their first departmental meeting, their curiosity and enthusiasm levels were off the chart. The opportunity to meet the other people Ivan had chosen to be in the group was also a highly anticipated event for each one of them. So when Ivan arrived at the meeting room he found his favorite operatives in a state of eager readiness.

"It's so nice to see you again," he began. "I can't hide the affection that I hold for each one of you. I've discussed the purpose of the Finders corps individually with you, and now it's time to pass out the first assignments."

Ivan distributed an envelope to each of those present and continued to speak. "What I'd like you to do is to take the dossier of citizen candidates that you find inside your envelopes, then I want you to think about how you're going to go about persuading these people that they should come to North America. Make a plan and call me for an appointment as soon as you think you're ready. Any questions?"

"I have a question," Colonel Cutler said.

"Yes, Craig, what is it?"

"May we invite the people on our list to come to the U.S.N.A. and meet the sponsor that got them to the list?"

"Yes, but only the ones you've qualified in your minds as being bona fide candidates to become good citizens in the event we invite them permanently into our country."

"That puts the onus on us, doesn't it Ivan?"

"Yes, but that's the challenge, isn't it? Each of you has been selected to do this job because somebody recognized various superior abilities in you."

"That someone couldn't have been you, could it?" The ironical question came from the only woman in the group, Commander Mary O'Neal.

"Well, Mary, you may be right, but that information is classified."

"I thought it might be, Ivan."

"My intention is to organize a targeted job fair, and once you've pinpointed the individuals we'd like to invite, we'll bring them to Washington en masse. It's more efficient to do it that way. In addition, if we can create a positive attitude among the invitees, then perhaps we can start an immigration stampede based on excellence—one that has an immediate effect on our economy, not one that involves random luck, long term investment, family nepotism or national biases. You must perform your individual recruiting assignments with the objective of simultaneously bringing all your candidates to the job fair in Washington six months from now. Any other questions before you trot off to deal with the information in the folders you've been given? No? Then I'll see each of you separately for a final briefing before you go operational."

When the meeting was over, Brooklyn entered Ivan's office as the others filed out.

"You seem to be treating the Finders' assignments as though they were spy missions," she observed.

"In a way they are," Ivan replied. "Just think about it, Brooklyn. Pretend you're the President of Pakistan, and imagine how he'll react when we persuade his chief nuclear scientist to skip off to North America to take a better job. We have to anticipate the worst, and we can't botch the deal by sending a lightweight to propose the deal and arrange the details of the defection."

"Well, my husband, Barry, is one of the Finders you're talking about. I don't want to have to consult the visiting hours at the jail in Medina in order to visit him."

"I think you're pissed off at me for asking him to join the Finders, aren't you Brooklyn?

"Yeah, who wouldn't be angry at the guy who put her husband's life in jeopardy?"

"Just remember that he volunteered for the assignment. He wasn't conscripted against his will. Furthermore, there's little danger for him in Latin America."

"That's easy to say, Ivan. But there are rough customers in Mexico, and Colombia too."

"True, but he's going to be recruiting economists and financiers, not soldiers, policemen, or politicians."

"Are you willing, then, to guarantee that Barry will be safe? You seem to be telling me that you're only going to send him on missions where his security is assured. Is this true? Can I depend on that?"

"You can depend on me to do my best not to expose him to trouble he can't handle, just as I'll do for all of our special agents. I must confess, Brooklyn, that it surprises me that you would ask that special consideration be given to anyone, including your husband. As far as I can recall, you didn't worry about my safety when I was in tight spots."

"Yes, but you're not the father of my children."

"I have a wife and children too, and you know that I wouldn't send anyone into danger without a full assessment of the risks involved. Our situation here and now is merely to offer certain highly regarded individuals an opportunity to join us in constructing the exceptional country that we hope the U.S.N.A. will become."

"I know it's always been your dream to improve our country and the world," Brooklyn said in a rather sharp tone of voice, "but most people are concerned with their own survival and that of their kids first, and the rest of the world second."

"That's the whole point, Brooklyn. Until we're just as concerned about other people's children as we are about our own, there'll be no improvement. The U.S.N.A. is not just an opportunistic attempt to strengthen North America, it's our chance to demonstrate to the world how and why it should follow our lead. To make that dream come true we need the wherewithal to do the job, and that's where the Finders come in. It's a challenge, but in the final analysis it's one that's worth giving up your life for. The Secretary of State thinks of the U.S.N.A. as the peace through prosperity plan for the nations of the world. The Finders know this, and they've agreed to accept the risks because the reward is worth it. Don't you see, Brooklyn? That's what President Quince is trying to accomplish, and we should all do whatever we can to help."

Brooklyn left Ivan's office to go back to her desk. She had been influenced, but not inspired. Her mother's love and family instincts were in conflict with the ideals of her boss. Until she had had children, Brooklyn would have followed Ivan's lead anywhere at any time, but now she wasn't sure if his leadership might not get her husband killed and make her children fatherless.

Ivan gave Brooklyn a reassuring pat on the shoulder and left his office to attend a meeting with Lorraine Plouffe, the Secretary of State. She had agreed to meet him for a short impromptu chat.

"Madame Secretary," he began, "I sought this little tête-à-tête so I can be sure we're on the same page before I send my Finders out into the world to do the President's work."

"Very well, Ivan, let's discuss the issues and see where we stand together and where we may differ."

"Well, I've just come from a meeting with my assistant, Brooklyn, whose husband is one of my new Finders special agents. During the discussion she questioned whether the danger to her husband was worth the risk to his person. Naturally, I took the positive position. First, I tried to calm her fears by telling her that since his background was as an IRS Special Agent, he'd only be recruiting economists and financial types, not politicians, and therefore there was little or no reason to worry about his personal welfare. Secondly, I told her that in any case, the work to be done by her husband would be worth the sacrifice, in the extremely unlikely event that he got into trouble in some foreign land. I just wondered whether you go along with me on this?"

"Well, I concur with your approach. After all, our motto here at the State Department is *Peace through Prosperity*. It supports the President's program for the U.S.N.A. perfectly, so anybody working for his goal is a hero. I recognize your assistant's right to be concerned about her family, however, but I assume her husband volunteered for the post, and being above the legal age of consent, he knew what he was doing. I suppose every woman left alone by a husband in the service has a degree of buyer's remorse, but she'll get over it."

"Thanks for the encouraging words, Lorraine. I hope you're right. This person has been with me a long time. I'd be very sorry to lose her. I'll give her time to come around. Now, I have a list for you of people by country that the Finders have been asked to recruit. I'd like to have any input or advice that you'd care to give before I send my agents into the field. Of course, the list will also give your departmental people some notice of our Finders' activity in several nations where we have embassies. I hope we can have the support of your embassy staff in the unlikely event that it's needed."

"Of course, Ivan, and thank you for the cooperation of your department. Too often the diplomatic problems we get into come from a lack of intradepartmental cooperation. We can't be of much use if we don't know what operations are underway in a foreign country, so we often appear to have egg on our face when things goes awry. I'll give you a list as soon as I can with the names specific embassy employees to match the countries where your Finders are operating. These diplomats will be specifically informed of the projects that are in progress, and they'll be asked to render any and all assistance that may be required."

"Thank you, Lorraine. And just so you know, I'm damn glad to have you Canadians aboard the good ship U.S.N.A."

This highly regarded, lifelong professional woman—a no-nonsense diplomat, immaculately dressed, handsome of face, trim of figure, multi-lingual and sixty years old—was surprised by the tall American's sincerely felt comment and his firm handshake as he left her office.

Olga's name on Cutler's list made Ivan Welland think once again about their brief acquaintance in their student days. He recalled how they had been observed playing chess together by a number of their colleagues as well as by some of the librarians. Eventually the chess fans among the students and faculty began to pay attention to their games. Somehow the idea of these two bright young people locked in cerebral conflict appealed to the people in the Math Department. The contest had several attractive aspects about it, especially since it was male vs. female, and Russia vs. the U.S.

Things around the Math Department usually tended to be unexciting, so a chess match between two of their stars was a welcome distraction, and an expectant buzz began to circulate. Eventually supporters sprang up to encourage the competitors. A few wagers were made about the outcome of the match, so Ivan and Olga were goaded into becoming public as well as private Cold War combatants.

Ivan was not very happy about the importance that his colleagues were placing on this little competition. He had not sought this type of notoriety, and the surfeit of comments from members of the Math Department in the event of a loss was distasteful to him. There was little to be gained by a victory, either, as far as any future badinage was concerned, since bragging would be seen as gauche. Backing out of the match was also not possible, as the perception of cowardice would be too great to bear. Of course it would all be jolly good fun for the spectators at the player's expense.

The clocks and the book of rules for international chess competitions quickly materialized. A three-game match was decided upon, and a referee appointed. The first contestant to win two games would be declared the winner of the Princeton Pea Pot, not to be confused with the Princeton Pee Pot, which was not being contested. Drawn games would be dropped. The games were to be played on two or more consecutive evenings, starting at eight o'clock sharp. The Math Department's largest seminar room would be the venue for the match. Graduate students, professors and staff, pledged to silence during play, would be the only spectators. Dress would be formal, as befitted the gentlemen and scholars of one of the foremost learning centers in the world.

Welland vs. Yukovich was shaping up as a heavyweight fight, but in actuality Ivan had never before played in a chess tournament. It was advantage Olga on that one. It was also advantage Olga in the games they had already played. The scorecard read 0-1-1 in her favor. If he had been a betting man he would have demanded odds to bet on himself. He was feeling the pressure of simulating the character of Ivan the Terrible, but he was surprised that at his core he wasn't really concerned. He knew that a game was just a game and nothing more. He was also trained from birth to do his best and leave the rest. Consequently he was emotionally relaxed, but his mind was in high gear. He recalled all the moves of the two games they had already played, and he felt familiar with her style of play. He noticed that she was strong in mind and audacity, but he felt that impatience and a certain lack of creativity were her weak points. He felt quite sure that if he could get her into uncharted waters he would triumph.

What a foolish idea, putting on formal dress clothes to play a game, he thought, as he clumsily tried to tie his bow tie. It was only the second time he had worn his tuxedo. The first time was when he was an usher at his sister's wedding, and his mother had helped him tie his tie on that occasion. Ivan liked tradition, so he was not entirely put off by the dress code, but he hoped that there was more to Ivy ethics than just the outward appearances.

"Here comes the biggest penguin in Christendom," he said to himself, and headed off to the Math Department.

When he appeared promptly at 7:50 he noticed that most of his colleagues had already arrived and had drinks in their hands. When they caught sight of Welland they delivered a polite round of applause and began taking their seats. The chessboard was on a table in the center of the room, and the spectators' seats surrounded it. The players were visible to most of the onlookers except those seated directly behind them. Welland would have preferred to have the room be a classroom with the chessboard in front of the blackboard. If this had been the case he could have averted his eyes when he was thinking or when he was waiting for Olga to make her move. With this theater-in-the round arrangement he might be distracted, no matter which way he looked.

Just then Olga arrived. She was wearing a long crimson floor-length gown, with a décolleté that could easily distract a male opponent as she bent over the board. Ivan chuckled. She looked like one of the Romanov girls at her engagement party, he thought. It was a good thing she had never won a gold medal at the Olympics, or she would have worn that too. She was using all the psychological weapons she could muster, which suggested to Ivan that she must be scared. She walked regally to the table, and Welland rose to meet her. He took her hand and kissed it, and bowed from the waist.

"Good evening Duchess," he said.

They seated themselves at the chessboard as the referee, also tuxedoed, stepped up to the table and said a few words of welcome. He briefly explained that the gameboard would be visually duplicated via a computer-generated projection onto a large screen along one wall of the room. A moveable blackboard had been placed on the opposite side of the room, and the game would be recorded on it in chess notation form for those who preferred to follow the moves in that way. He announced that the question of who would play white or black would be decided by a coin toss. He flipped the coin and in the best football tradition, asked Olga, the visitor, to call heads or tails while the coin was in the air. She called heads. The coin came up heads, so she chose to play white. In future matches the advantage of first move would rotate back and forth. Ivan was then allowed to decide at which side of the board to sit. He chose the side facing the screen. He preferred to watch the screen, which was an exact duplicate of the board itself, and thus offered no distraction. The referee, having done his job, shook hands with Ivan and Olga and wished them good luck. Olga opened with a Queen's Pawn game.

This first match between Yukovich and Welland began a new tradition. Each year a woman and a man from among the entering graduate students in mathematics are selected, by a vote of their peers, to compete for the Pea Pot. The name of the winner is emblazoned in pea green-colored ink across the front of the pot. The first Pea Pot contained soil with a single pea planted in it. It is the responsibility of each year's chess winner to grow the plant and supply the seed pea for the next year. Many Pea Pot champions have since done it.

Welland was in the most cheerful of moods when Olga's queen pawn opening indicated she would be in her usual daring attack mode when playing white. He knew he would be spending the next hour beating back her every thrust and parry. If he made no mistakes and was patient, he could turn the tide and organize a counter attack. Probably it would be inelegant, but a win would take the heart out of her.

During the end game Olga knew that she was going to lose, so she laid down her king and resigned. With her face flushed nearly as red as her dress, she extended her hand so that Ivan could shake it, but he quickly grasped it and kissed it as before.

"Thank you for the brave game, Countess," he said. The knowledgeable spectators applauded and let out a roar of appreciation. Nobody in the room noticed that Ivan had demoted Olga from duchess to countess. The chess aficionados in the audience did realize, however, that Welland had essentially become an expert chess player in only six weeks.

The next night Olga arrived in a high neck, white three-quarter length dress. Ivan thought this indicated that she was trying to be cool and collected. She would need to be, for he had a creative plan of attack in mind for his white pieces that he hoped would show her why she had never become a great chess player. He began with a cautious opening which Olga interpreted as weakness, just as Ivan had expected. She fell right into his trap, and before she knew it she was put in an impossible position and forced to resign again. This time his victory was elegant, rapier-like, and overwhelming.

"Thank you Baroness, playing chess with you has been one of the highlights of my life."

Olga knew now that this young man was someone to be respected. She particularly felt disarmed by his humility, because he had not evinced one ounce of superiority in his voice and manner when he thanked her for a great game, although she knew perfectly well that he knew better. Olga hated losing. She adopted a stance of good sportsmanship, but in her heart she craved revenge and resented his modesty. Had this been Russia, and she the victor, she would have oozed unabashed superiority. They left the room arm-in-arm to show the spectators that there were no hard feelings.

CHAPTER FIVE

Colonel Craig Cutler was the perfect picture of a military officer. He was tall, fit, and rugged. Some would have said he was handsome, but in truth his nose was a bit too large, his mouth too small, and his eyes too deeply set to conform to the Hollywood standard of good looks. As he stood at the entrance to Ivan's office he felt a bit foolish wearing a business suit, but it was not possible for him to perform his present mission in military dress. He was going overseas as a representative of his government, but not as an Army officer. Distinguished, successful businessperson was the image he was expected to project. In truth he was nearing the end of his active duty, and this assignment with the Finders was calculated to help him make the transition to civilian employment.

Cutler had enlisted in the U.S. Army as a buck private right out of high school. He hadn't exactly knocked them dead in school, as he had been more interested in playing football and basketball. He had performed well on both his school's teams, but not well enough to be recruited by any name colleges. So he enlisted in the Army where he had found his true métier. His natural intelligence, common sense, and wide-ranging interests took root in the manly soil of Army life, so as a result he was frequently promoted and offered entrance to special courses.

When he was chosen for training as a helicopter pilot he was almost beside himself with joy. It is a little-known fact that the Army employs more helicopter pilots than the Air Force. This is because the helicopter has become the modern Army's cavalry horse and its airborne tank. In addition to close-in attack air support, tactical troops are ferried every-where these days by choppers, and the wounded are brought out the same way. At the completion of the pilot's course, Craig Cutler was routinely promoted to warrant officer, which is the highest enlisted man's rank. After a year of sterling service in that grade he was promoted to lieutenant and made the transition to junior officer.

What boosted his military career further was an incident that took place in the early days of fighting in Afghanistan. While engaged in ferrying special forces to a hotspot, he set his chopper down in the courtyard of a building, released his cargo of infantry, and was preparing to lift off to make his next run when he noticed an abandoned box of ammunition sitting unobtrusively in a corner of the building. Almost on a whim, Cutler ordered his crewman to retrieve the wooden box and bring it aboard. The crate was imprinted with Chinese characters on several sides. When Cutler returned to his base he took the box to his commanding officer.

"Sir, I wonder if I could make a tactical suggestion," he began.

"What is it, Cutler?"

"We retrieved this crate of enemy ammo on our last mission, and I think we should return it to them."

"What the hell are you talking about?"

"Well sir, what if we manufactured some ammunition and put it in crates just like this one, with the writing and all, but instead of their live ammo we replaced it with some booby trapped ammo that resembled theirs, but which would be made to explode in the faces of those who used it?"

"That's brilliant, Cutler. I'll talk to our Black Ops guys and see if it can be done."

It was done, and in a number of instances it proved to be successful. Cutler received a medal and a promotion to captain as a result. This promotion put him on the fast track in the ranks of the commissioned officers. It also gained him entrance to training courses at which he excelled. These included Black Ops and Special Forces tactics. It was at this stage in his career that he met Ivan Welland, who was then

Secretary of Defense. Ivan was superlative at recognizing potential early in a man's career. Cutler's ordinary academic accomplishments belied his true abilities, but he surmounted this deficiency and was given command of a helicopter unit and promoted to the rank of major. Later Major Cutler was given command of a helicopter training unit in which he oversaw pilot training until he was made a bird colonel and sent to the war college to take courses that would lead to his being made a full colonel. It was at this point in his distinguished career that he received the call that would see him allocated to Welland's new Finders unit.

Cutler was a soldier created to interdict the new enemies that no longer fought as national armies. During his time in the military the enemy combatants fought in cells that were not clearly connected to a hierarchy of command. No longer were they to be found in major mechanized units under the orders of a central corps of identifiable leaders. Today's military men had to root out terrorist insurgents that were not in uniform. The opponents of the military now blended in with the general populations, and used the local people for cover. Strangely enough the inhabitants, instead of feeling victimized, permitted the insurgents to operate in their midst, granted them status as heroes and martyrs, and secretly hoped they would win out over the infidel foreigners with whom they conducted business. Cleverness, chicanery, and guile were the weapons with which the terrorists attempted to overthrow western civilization. To the extent they could afford it, the decentralized extremists also used technology to wage their battles, but more often they dealt out death in the form of cheap improvised explosive devices. Partly by coincidence and partly by perception, Cutler was a poster boy for the modern soldier.

Ivan recognized that Cutler was a prototypical modern army officer, but his interest in him had more to do with his personal sang-froid, intelligence, and integrity. He had seen him in action, partnered with him to overcome obstacles, and

trusted his instincts. As a result Ivan felt that he should be
assigned to contact those individuals that we most wanted to
be on our side in any conflict that might arise. His audience
would be those officers with exceptional military minds, and
those with advanced technical and tactical knowledge. Anyone in this category would be of great value to the U.S.N.A.
as well as a great loss to those countries with large military
and industrial establishments whose intentions toward the
U.S.N.A. were not clearly fraternal and pacific. In Cutler's
case, this meant spending time in Russia and China.

Cutler's list of targets for recruitment by the Finders was
compiled with the input of the CIA, military intelligence,
corporations, universities, and the State Department. The
candidates on the list were suggested by executives, officers
and government officials in various U.S.N.A. departments
with reference to candidates who might make good compatriots and who could supply desired special knowledge, skills
in short supply, or specific experience required to assist with
the expansion of President Quince's new unity for progress.
The principal targets of the Finders agents were candidates
that would regard it as an honor to be invited to live in North
America and share in the grand future that was developing.

The decisions about inviting candidates to the U.S.N.A.
would be left up to Cutler. The Colonel would be officially
classified as a high-level civilian American executive. His
contacts with candidates selected for special immigration
would be informal, but because his listed immigrants were
being recruited and not just casually accepted out of a spirit
of mercy, they would be entitled to special status. Thus
Cutler would be empowered to offer them some enticing
compensations in the form of employment, transportation,
quick citizenship and voting rights.

In going over Cutler's list with him, Ivan had decided
not to interfere or mention that he knew one of the persons
on the list. After all, Cutler might not choose Olga Yukovich
as one of the Finders' keepers, or she might decline his invi-

tation if he offered her the chance to come to the U.S.N.A. Besides, Cutler had decided to focus first on candidates that had high-level experience with geology opportunities in the far North. His first contacts would be with oil and mineral technology specialists. Olga's résumé appeared to place her outside Cutler's primary focus group. If it came down to final acceptance or rejection, only then would Welland assert his authority.

During the next few days Ivan spent his time going over the lists of other Finders as he had done with Colonel Cutler's list. In preparing the assignments, he had tried to capitalize on matching his Finders' individual talents and experiences to their recruitment targets. He paid special attention to the national origin of the targeted people on the lists. In selecting the targets, inability to speak English was a disqualifying criterion—no English, no invitation to the U.S.N.A. It was as simple as that. The union of Canada and the United States had been enormously complicated, almost to the point of failure, because the majority of the population at first did not grasp the absolute necessity for having the unifying benefit of a common language, and that language had to be English. Ivan's decision was not in any way meant to debase other languages—it was just a simple fact that English was the lingua franca of most of the world at that time in history.

Opponents of the merger of the two nations had fought like wildcats over the issue of retaining French and Spanish. Quince, before he was elected, had to prove to a majority of the voters that he had no intention of forcing people to speak English in their homes, but he had to prove to the electorate how advantageous it was for a modern nation to at least have a single official written language. In his speeches he had cited the tremendously unifying effect that using English had had on India. The people of India spoke a large number of different languages and had many dialects, but what united them was the salubrious result of the occupation of their country by Britain, and the necessity of learning English in order to communicate with the government. In the modern world the English language had advanced the population of India tremendously. Few Indians would argue the point, although having to live under foreign rule in order to gain success as a nation had been a tough pill to swallow.

Similar stories during his campaign for the presidency were recounted by Quince to demonstrate the essential point that one language had to be used and understood by all the citizens if a modern nation were to succeed. He pointed out how Turkey had risen out of the Middle East in the 20th century as a result of Kemal Ataturk's insistence on the use of Roman letters in place of Arabic script. Chairman Mao Zedong also unified his country partly thanks to the one written official script that was universally understood by the entire Chinese populace. Although many of these turbulent times were far from ideal, they were essential in assisting these nations to achieve their present status, and the catalyst was the adoption of a unifying language.

The practicality of English as a primary language won out, and the supporters of dissension were defeated. Quince and Welland had discussed this problem in depth, and had decided that they had to face the language issue head on. The plan to build the U.S.N.A. into a strong nation couldn't be delayed while one or two generations of new immigrants learned English and assimilated the North American culture. For that reason immigration would have to be suspended until it was a clearly accepted policy that all citizens and all immigrants have a good grasp of English. No new citizens would be accepted by the administration of the U.S.N.A. until they passed an English language test, and no voters would be able to vote without their demonstrating a good knowledge of English.

Since this one-language policy was a plank in Quince's platform from the time he arrived on the political scene, it also had to be an essential criterion of the Finders' mission statement. Therefore all interviews with candidates seeking admission to the U.S.N.A. had to be conducted in English by the Finders agents. Generally speaking this meant that the candidates had to have spent some time in the United States or Canada. Usually they had studied English as students in their home country, and then had polished their skills and fluency in North American universities. Some extensive practice using English as a second language was essential for fast-tracking new citizen candidates. Background checking was also much easier if they had spent some time in North America. It was a well-documented fact that many students came to Western universities with a good reading knowledge of English, but they were unable to speak or be understood because the language teachers in their home countries had not mastered spoken English themselves, and were therefore unable to teach it properly to others.

Chinese and other Asian students were essentially the victims of a lack of exposure to the proper pronunciation of English. Since good work habits were a common attribute of Asian students, statistics showed that more Asians were presently studying English than there were native speakers of English in North America. Large numbers of Americans and Canadians were going to Asia to teach English and address the problem of poor pronunciation and poor comprehension. The trouble was that with respect to teaching English these young adventurers in education were qualified only by the fact that they were native speakers of English whose main desire was to see the world and meet foreigners.

Ivan had made his views about these matters clear to his Finders. He insisted that a high level of English comprehension be basic to all those candidates being considered for the special treatment offered by the Finders corps. The political correctness people were up in arms about the discriminatory potential implied in the search for candidates with fluency in English, but Quince and Welland were adamant.

Ivan chose Finders agents instead of picking linguists to do the job because he wanted to get a quick return on his investment in the people chosen by the Finders. He was not interested in setting up a Rosetta Stone school for foreigners. He sought people who were prepared to go to work in their chosen fields as soon as they arrived in North America, and his method was to put bright, practical people in charge of deciding who were the most suitable for fast assimilation. He would be responsible for the decisions about whom to admit to the country, and he would take the flak that went with the job, but he would not compromise President Quince's desire to energize the economy by providing it with an influx of highly qualified people, especially in the critical formative stages of the U.S.N.A. The Finders program was not to be a training program for speaking and understanding English—it was meant to be an intensive recruitment search for leaders in essential fields of endeavor who already had an excellent command of the language.

Ivan made this perfectly clear to his corps of recruiters, so as he worked his way through the dossiers of his Finders, he didn't mind telling them why they had been selected to go where they were being sent, and why they were the best choice to recruit in that particular area, and why they were the most qualified to succeed with the specific people to whom they had been assigned. Welland saw himself as the V.P. of International Sales for the U.S.N.A. He was sure he had the best product to sell, and he couldn't even imagine why anyone in his right mind wouldn't want to participate in what he regarded as the best opportunity on the planet to achieve freedom and prosperity. He was expecting dramatic results from his Finders, and it was with great optimism that he was engaged in the planning stages of each and every recruitment attempt.

That day he was going over dossiers with Commander Mary O'Neal, U.S.N. She had been a student/scholar in high school at the time she learned that she had been accepted as a midshipman at the United States Naval Academy in Annapolis, Maryland. Her acceptance in the august institution struck her as a bit strange, since just about the only sport she hadn't tried was sailing. She had never been excited by the thought of long imprisonments on ships at sea, so when it came to choosing her elective courses she had opted for the ones least apt to be nautical. Her interests and her athleticism led her to the Seals as a first choice, Intelligence as a second choice, and to the business end of running the Navy as a third preference. In the course of completing her four years at the Academy she had done studies and internships in all three areas, and her instructors had rated her as excellent all along the way. She graduated near the top of her class, was given her commission as an ensign in the United States Navy, and was posted to active duty.

Her first assignment was to get through the Navy Seal training course. Women had done it before, but not many tried and fewer succeeded. Mary, however, was from a large family and most of her siblings were brothers, so she was experienced at competing with men. She was strong for a woman, but she estimated that even the strongest woman was at least 15% weaker than the average healthy, athletic man. Mary didn't fool herself about being as strong as a man, but she knew that nothing was stopping her from being smarter. She spent a good deal of her physical training time devoted to martial arts theory, and she mastered the use of leverage, speed, and turning the force of an opponent's attack back against him. She was naturally competitive and excelled in all team sports. Unfortunately all the emphasis that she had placed on competing with men had left her unprepared for relationships based on sexual attraction. The fact that she was highly intelligent and outshone most of her male companions had also discouraged potential suitors from approaching her in spite of her female beauty. What few dates she had accepted in high school and at the Academy had resulted in some clumsy and unmemorable incidents that left her unenthusiastic about the sensibilities of the opposite sex.

Ivan first encountered Mary after she had been in the Navy long enough to have been promoted to Lieutenant J.G. She had been Captain John Mercer's second-in-command in the Navy Seal detail during the cruise ship incident. Ivan recalled that she was an extremely competent young officer. He admired her pluck, but it was her intelligence that had captivated him and had caused him to place her name in his memory bank to be recalled should ever the need arise. Ivan made a mental note to interview her as soon as possible, for John Mercer had recommended her for a position in Great Britain. The U.K. was one of the strongest allies of the U.S.N.A., so the recruiting issue was especially touchy. Ivan didn't want to be seen as attempting to recruit their best people away from them, so the Finder for this area would have to be intelligent, tactful, and sensitive to the feelings of others. Captain Mercer was convinced that Mary O'Neal was the perfect candidate for the job.

CHAPTER SIX

Ivan's next meeting was with Captain John Mercer. Ivan always wondered if a romance would spring up between Mary O'Neal and Mercer. It seemed to him that they were a couple meant for each other. He felt a bit let down when he found out that the U.S. Navy had unintentionally stymied any incipient relationship that might otherwise have occurred by stationing Mercer in San Diego and O'Neal in NATO Headquarters in Europe. Both had been so career-oriented that they had not fanned the spark they both felt when they had been on assignment with Welland aboard the Controller of the Oceans. They both had been conscious of the attraction that existed between them, but neither could take the initiative because of their career professionalism. This, in spite of the fact that they were delegated to play the part of a married vacationing couple on board the ship as part of the cover story that Ivan Welland had arranged to foil the terrorist plot that might have sunk the largest passenger ship in the world.

Captain John Mercer was scheduled to do his recruiting work in Australia and New Zealand. The same subtleties and restrictions applied to this task as had pertained to Mary O'Neal's recruiting assignment in the U.K. They were not to jeopardize the diplomatic relationship between the U.S.N.A. and the few friendly nations that could be trusted. Ivan and the Captain discussed the matter thoroughly during their last meeting. It was made crystal clear that Mercer should imme-diately abandon any recruitment effort that threatened the relationship between good allies in any way.

Mercer had managed to stay single in spite of the hard-fought efforts of several intelligent and ambitious women to cull him from the ranks of the unmarried. His parents had hoped that he would marry, settle down, and give them some grandchildren to spoil, but now that John was forty they were losing this hope. Mary was battling her parents over the same problem—when would she marry and procreate? Both Mary and John in the past had recognized the mating potential of the other, but so much time had sped by that neither had been able to think about rekindling the relationship. It eventually became a question of out of sight, out of mind. It seemed ironic to them that their first work assignment together was to pretend they were married, yet all their assignments thereafter had prevented them from ever seeing each other again. After years of separation, however, they met again at the behest of Ivan Welland. Their reunion had been a pleasant surprise, but they knew that life in the military was often a series of meetings and partings, so neither John nor Mary took it as anything other than a normal career coincidence.

Ivan's orientation sessions with those he had chosen to be the first Finder Special Agents had brought the two bright naval officers together again, but they both knew that their assignments would soon take them to different continents. As a result they were tentative about beginning a relationship that would almost immediately take them out of each other's orbit once again. They did have a catch-up dinner together during their time in Washington, but their conversation was kept pretty much exclusively on the topic of business. Both John and Mary were vaguely conscious that their association could be more than just business, but it was obvious that it would be useless to pursue it in the light of their impending assignments, so they refrained from letting their attraction develop beyond friendship.

Ivan's avuncular interest in these two was aroused again. He would have liked to see Mercer and O'Neal become a domestic team as well as a patriotic dynamic duo, but his role as Cupid was countermanded by his responsibility to the President to accomplish his mission of developing a targeted immigration policy on the basis of the merit of an individual applicant instead of letting it remain a passive one whereby the U.S.N.A. would merely wait and accept any and nearly all who opportunistically applied for green cards. Although Ivan was aware of a certain desire on his part to see these two get together, he also knew that it was his job to send them far away from each other. At this time, however, all he could do was promise himself to put them into another close working situation if the opportunity arose.

Ivan's meeting with Barry Mendelson was a different matter. Barry was Brooklyn's husband, and next to his wife Marina and their daughter, she was the most important woman in Ivan's life. She had been with him since the day he arrived back from Chechnya and settled into his first job at the State Department. She had eased him into the Washington scene, covering his naiveté with her competency and insider's knowledge. She had developed along with him and had become all she could be alongside his meteoric rise in government. Now, however, a rift had developed between them because Ivan was sending Barry away from her on a dangerous mission.

Ivan had brokered the marriage between Brooklyn and Barry in a sense, and the couple thought of him as some sort of gentile catalyst of good fortune, but now Brooklyn was having second thoughts about Ivan's priorities. How could he give and then take away her husband as though he were Jehovah? She was less than sure that the Finder program was a sound one, and she didn't want to be separated from her husband over a policy that might, in her opinion, go bust. She and Ivan had occasionally had differences, but nothing on the scale of this one. She was a typically liberal New Yorker, and he was a conservative Texan. They had always surmounted their basically opposing views by placing the nation's safety issues ahead of their personal leanings. This time Brooklyn felt that the immigration issue was divisive, and that in principal it had little merit. Soliciting talented immigrants was counter to her vision of providing a home for the despondent and oppressed immigrants who, like her parents, had come through Ellis Island, passing by the Statue of Liberty en route. Brooklyn was sure that substituting merit for mercy as the central issue in immigration policy was just plain wrong.

Brooklyn had made her position clear to Ivan, but he had chosen to ignore it. He argued that the new nation formed by the merger of Canada and the United States called for fast action to amalgamate the two entities, especially in the spheres of science and economics. His position was that the new nation couldn't afford to wait for a generation or two of immigrants to become educated and take up the slack. Ivan felt that the U.S.N.A. was most vulnerable to outside forces during the settling in period. He felt experts were needed to head off the ambitions of opposition foreign forces that would sense the confusion and vulnerability of the giant that was emerging in the West. Ivan was certain that after the new nation was on a firm footing, its immigration policy could be reformed or returned to its previous existence, but for the moment he remained adamant that the Finders corps was the way to go. And as far as Barry was concerned, Ivan felt he was his own man and could accept or reject the assignment as he pleased. He had chosen to accept it, and that was good enough for Ivan, and anyway he was only sending him to New Zealand and Australia for the time being, and those countries were allies and safe for North American visitors and businessmen.

Taxes are always a hot button issue among democracies. Tax policy is usually where the rubber hits the road where the government of the people is concerned. Nobody wants to pay taxes. Giving away hard-earned money to some anonymous government bureaucrats is anathema to one and all, but everyone recognizes that taxes are a necessary evil. No one better understands the ins and outs, the good and the bad, of the tax system than an Internal Revenue agent. Barry was the ultimate IRS man when it came down to it. Ivan needed

Barry's practical knowledge of taxation as it had been, and as it should be in the future, so that he could structure the tax policies of the U.S.N.A. The two men knew for certain it was going to be a hard slog to get the new entity into a position to handle its joint finances, and they regarded it as essential that they get all the knowledgeable assistance they could muster from wherever in the world they could find it. On this issue and at this time, the men in her life battered Brooklyn down, but she was determined to rise bloody and undefeated from the conflict. The men had to agree to hear her out again at a later time. Barry was therefore cleared to take the Finder's position, but only by the skin of his teeth.

Ivan Welland had parlayed his Harvard degree into a unique career. The benefits of his education had also redounded to the fame of the institution as he progressed through the ranks of politics and government. As a result of this reciprocation, Ivan had kept in close contact with the famous thinkers that populated his alma mater. He had even been instrumental in seeing to it that several of his associates received appointments to teach there. Ivan was a realist, however, and he expected Harvard to be an academic haven, not a heaven on earth. As a result of his predisposition to admire the educational possibilities of Harvard, he was disappointed with the quality of the new ideas coming out of that august university, particularly those coming from the departments of political science, history, and government. He expected the graduate degree program to advance the current borders of research by studying and suggesting improvements that could strengthen and ameliorate the way nations governed themselves and cooperated with one another. Instead what he found was a rather mundane effort to seek grants that were to be used to persuade the world that the U.S.N.A. had all the answers, and the rest of the world should simply follow along in its wake. Since that was not about to happen, however, the policies introduced by President Quince had to revolutionize what it meant to work for the new administration.

Ivan was determined to see to it that civil service jobs in the U.S.N.A. would no longer be lifelong sinecures that attracted mostly those who valued security above all else. A career with the government had to become the first choice of the majority of job seekers, and why not? Wasn't the government supposed to lead the nation's progress into the future? Eventually even the government employee unions would be forced to admit that obligatory opposition to any policies that sought to change the combative collective bargaining roles was pure foolishness. When the wages and benefits that the government was offering its employees were at par with those of equivalent workers in the private sector, the klieg lights would focus on the self-serving unions, and their popularity with the workers they claimed to serve would decline. Once the unions were exposed, their union-shop gangster tactics would be reviled, and dues-paying union membership would drop off precipitously. When the union members realized that they already had higher pay and more benefits than anyone else, union membership would become moot. At this point Secretary Welland would be able to revamp the entire U.S. Civil Service code without massive interference from the public service workers unions.

Ivan began thinking about the two men who would be best suited to help him in this endeavor. Byron Begley and Mike Dickerson represented the legal profession in the Finders crew. Begley's career growth began in the F.B.I. and had been due to his tremendous investigative abilities, which had led the government to recover billions of dollars of TARP funds that were about to be illegally moved offshore. Begley's intervention halted the biggest attempted swindle in history, and was described in the bestselling novel, *The Usury Suspects*. Begley was appointed to be a U.S. attorney following in the footsteps of Mike Dickerson, whose route had also taken him from the F.B.I. to the department of the

Attorney General. Dickerson had been Begley's boss at the F.B.I., and together they had prosecuted the executives of the political parties that had conspired to pull off the voter frauds that could have resulted in ending the American electoral system. Ivan's plan to use these two investigators as Finders was a stroke of genius and a bit of good luck.

It was Ivan's idea that Begley and Dickerson, with their legal backgrounds and familiarity with the U.S. Constitution, could be used to search the world for some new thinkers to expand the programs at Harvard and other elite institutions. Ivan had long felt that mankind had periodically become frozen in its allegiance to various governmental forms as they existed at certain times. Thus the concepts that created kingdoms, empires, and even democracies were tainted by formations in the past. They never allowed for transitions to the future, with the possible exception of the United States Constitution. That document, through its specified amending procedures, anticipated the possibility of growth and change, and therefore it gives some hope for a future that can develop peacefully. The continuum of life would not be stopped, for Ivan believed it is the will of the Creator that it go on, and that it is the responsibility of mankind to learn how to provide for a peaceful future.

Ivan's meeting with Begley and Dickerson would be somewhat different than the ones that had taken place with the other Finder agents. In the first place, the two legal experts would not be told whom to recruit. They would have to root out their own candidates by researching the political writings of men and women from all over the world. Usually these people were unpopular with their governments because they advocated change. This meant that much of their work might be intentionally buried by the powers that be. Digging out an incipient Gandhi or any relatively unknown foreign political philosopher would not be easy, but that was the challenge that Ivan gave his legal duo. The job would require studying the writings and speeches of dissenting thinkers, most of which would need translating before the works could be evaluated. Ivan thought that David Feingold's computer skills could be a big help to Begley and Dickerson, so he had him sit in on the meeting.

They all agreed with Ivan that the first stop should be the State Department, which keeps pertinent information on every country in the world. Ivan called Lorraine Plouffe to obtain clearance for his Finders to interview her regional under-secretaries and consult their files. Plouffe was always interested in what Ivan was up to. He was regarded by most of the Cabinet Members as something of a loose cannon, but Lorraine, an ex-Canadian, had no previous business dealings with Ivan prior to the formation of the U.S.N.A., so she had no preconceived notions about him. Her first impressions of him had been very positive, and in fact he was her favorite Cabinet colleague.

After Ivan explained to her exactly what he was trying to do with the information he needed, she became her usual cooperative self. She immediately saw the benefits to her own department of having a computerized summary of the governments of every nation on the planet in one data bank such as the one Ivan was proposing. Meetings between their lieutenants were set up to arrange for the interchange of information concerning inter-departmental communications.

Ivan knew that patriotism would be the main objection that leaders and dissenters from other countries would have about their compatriots coming to the U.S.N.A. Welland had always hated blind allegiance to any dicta, whether political or religious. When he read a book by Aidan de Vries called *U.S.N.A.: The United States of North America*, he felt that at long last someone had put patriotism in its proper place. He began his meeting with Dickenson and Begley by reading them a passage from the book that had started Ivan thinking about the Finders in the first place.

"Stephen Decatur," he read, "the American naval hero is quoted as having said, *Our country! In her intercourse with foreign nations may she always be in the right; but our country, right or wrong.* John Quincy Adams, known by his peers as *Old Man Eloquent* is quoted as having written in response, *May our country be always successful, but whether successful or otherwise, always right.* That's better, but best of all on this topic is this paraphrase of a quote attributed to G.K. Chesterton: *My country right or wrong is the equivalent of saying my mother; drunk or sober."*

"I want you two gentlemen to find me some political philosophers with open, creative minds," Welland continued. "They need to be writers whose thinking is original. People who describe what a government should be, and which will stand up to harsh criticism."

"I get you Ivan, but birds like that are rare," Begley said.

"They're an endangered species," Dickerson agreed.

"Well, your job is to find out if any still exist, and if you find one, convince him or her to come to North America and infect us with that rare politically incorrect disease caused by the apertopsychophagic virus."

"Excuse me boss, but what's that?" Begley asked.

"It's a word I made up to make open-mindedness sound important. Don't take me too seriously, Byron. Too many years in Widener Library at Harvard causes linguists to go berserk and start inventing new words, always long ones with Latin and Greek derivations. In the meantime I'll ask Feingold to work up an algorithm and write a computer program that will serve, first as a template for data entry, and eventually as an analytical tool to help you zero in on your quarry, so to speak. Now, gentlemen, we've got work to do, so let's get started."

While Ivan's meetings with various other Finders were being held in Washington, the first reports from the three Finder agents already in the field were beginning to trickle in. Ivan had hoped that Craig Cutler, who had made Russia his first stop, would not find Olga Yukovich to be a suitable recruitment candidate. Unfortunately, Cutler was impressed with her and wanted to send her to the U.S. for follow-up interviews prior to making her an offer of citizenship in the U.S.N.A. Ivan knew her to be competitive, immoral, selfish, and untrustworthy, but he didn't want to have to impugn her character unless it became absolutely necessary. He decided to let things proceed to the next step. He reasoned that he could kill the invitation at the last minute if he wished, but perhaps she would flunk out along the way and his negative intervention would be unnecessary. Welland didn't know how advanced she had become in her career as a computer engineer, and his opinions were based purely on his personal observations.

Ivan didn't want to inhibit Cutler's initiative by unduly criticizing his first recruitment effort. As long as no final decision about Olga's candidacy had yet been made, he could go along with Colonel Cutler's procedures. There was, of course, the unlikely possibility that Olga had changed. It would be interesting, if nothing else came of it, to see how the intervening years had affected her. Welland had been interfacing with the world's leaders, and he admitted that he might have become jaundiced about the probability of any of them falling prey to a transforming experience. Nevertheless, using Alexander Pope's theory that hope springs eternal in the human breast, Ivan Welland decided to leave the door of his cynicism open a crack to see if a drop of wisdom had somehow penetrated Olga's egocentricity.

CHAPTER SEVEN

With the merger of the United States and Canada, combined with the defection of the nations that chose to become independent after the dissolution of the USSR, Russia was no longer the largest country on the planet Earth. Many of her most important political, military, industrial, and criminal figures bitterly resented this decline, and they took out their vitriol on the new successor giant in the West. Naturally, with her overblown competitive spirit, Olga Yukovich was one of those who took the formation of the U.S.N.A. as a personal defeat.

Ever since her time at Princeton, Olga had followed in her father's footsteps. She had taken on the identity of a computer engineer, but that was a cover for her real career in the Secret Police. In actuality she had become an undercover officer in the most prestigious unit of the FSB, the successor organization to the Soviet era KGB, and the equivalent of the U.S. Department of Homeland Security. She had done many covert assignments, handling special tasks in espionage and counterintelligence. Her supposed expertise was in the field of computer applications as used in petroleum drilling in the Arctic, but her real value to Russia was as a spy.

Colonel Cutler thought that Olga's experience might be useful to the U.S.N.A. companies that were expanding their operations in Alaska and Alberta. He didn't know that Olga Yukovich had been carefully following the career of Ivan Welland ever since their days at Princeton. Welland's idea of targeted immigration was no secret, and when Olga learned about it she contrived through her connections in the Foreign Intelligence Service to get her name to appear on the list of candidates for immigration to the U.S.N.A.

Preparing a counterfeit curriculum vitae was no trouble for the forged documents department of the FSB. Leaders left over from the Cold War period still operated out of the same foreboding building in Moscow's downtown Lubyanka Square. Russia maintained the largest staff of uniformed and civilian espionage operatives in the world, numbering over a quarter of a million persons and, with the possible exception of Israel, probably the best-trained black ops intelligence operatives on the planet.

Ivan couldn't blame the Colonel for being taken in by this scam, for on the surface Olga appeared to be a perfect candidate to assist North America to accomplish its stated goal of becoming independent of imported oil. Knowing Olga as he did, Ivan was suspicious. In the first place, as far as he could see, Ivan couldn't find any indication that Olga had ever been anywhere North of St. Petersburg. This wasn't a good sign for a person claiming to be an expert in Arctic oil exploration, drilling, and refining. As far as Ivan knew, the main thrust of the developing Russian petroleum industry was in the Caspian Sea basin, and not in the Arctic regions. Even so, he was ready to let the arrangements continue for her trip to the U.S.N.A. to be interviewed by the Finders, if only so that he could determine what she was really up to.

Several others on Cutler's list had declined lucrative offers to come to North America on the pretext of wanting to remain in their homeland with their families. These refusals of Colonel Craig's initial offers seemed more reasonable to Ivan than had Olga's immediate acceptance. Her overly quick response reminded Ivan of her aggressive mode in chess playing, where her fierce attention to offense left her vulnerable when confronted by a sturdy defense. He sensed something was amiss in her willingness to suddenly uproot herself and come to North America, and he vowed to keep a close watch on her to determine her intentions. Something deep inside him predicted that the old chess game with Olga would never end until she won decisively, or died trying.

Meanwhile in the Middle East Captain John Mercer, an ex U.S. Navy Seal, was having trouble with his recruiting efforts. The principal hang-up with his Finder offers was not in determining who should receive these offers, but mostly concerned the vulnerabilities of family members should the candidate accept an offer from the U.S.N.A. Highly trained individuals in the most advanced scientific occupations were not exempt from retaliations against relatives remaining in the home country. Government officials and religious leaders immediately brought threats and pressures to bear on anyone thinking of jumping ship. Fear of a fatwa was the weapon of choice for those who opposed the individual's freedom of career choice. Anyone thinking of leaving the country faced assassination personally, or the torture and murder of loved ones left behind.

Cultural practices were another factor that influenced Mercer to change his approach to his Arab recruitment targets. Islamic religious custom militated against a Muslim functioning in a mostly Christian society, but those who were already in North America working or going to school were a different matter. Students particularly, having had a taste of life in the West, might more likely be tempted to remain and work in the U.S.N.A. Mercer was convinced that his part in the Finder's program should be changed to reflect this fact. In the case of Arab nationals, he preferred to persuade talented students already in North America to remain in place after graduation. He communicated these feelings to Welland, and together they began to work on an organized early identification system that could shine the spotlight of opportunity on Muslim candidates who in the future might become leaders in industry.

Commander Mary O'Neal was having none of the problems that her senior naval officer, Captain Mercer, was facing. Generally speaking the British, particularly the Scots and the Irish, were very interested in migrating to North America if a lucrative offer was made. The merger of Canada and the United States into the U.S.N.A. had been received in the United Kingdom with both admiration and opportunism. Centuries of migrations had mentally prepared the British for relocations. Underlying and undermining the unity of the British Isles was the centuries-old political and religious strife that promoted the desire for independence. For this reason Mary wasn't facing the problems with her candidate list that her colleague John was having in the Middle East.

The irony of the modern age of technology is that the efficiencies brought about by inventions meant to reduce work and improve performance are more than balanced out by the increased costs of developing those technologies. As a result of these spiraling expenses, corporations had to raise huge amounts of capital to fund the R&D and start-up costs necessary to produce the new technologies; these investment costs were met by mergers, acquisitions, stock issues, and the formation of huge international conglomerates that could afford, or could borrow, the enormous amounts of capital required to stoke the fires of constant technological growth. The most successful corporations in the world were truly international in their scope. Workers at all levels were aware of the big name companies in their sectors of the economy.

Commander Mary O'Neal was finding it easy to contact the people on her list in the U.K., and to discuss openly the opportunities being offered by companies functioning in the rapidly expanding economy of the U.S.N.A. What made it easier was the relaxation of the long immigration formalities due to Welland's Finders program of targeted immigration. Of course it was helpful for Mary to be able to function in English with applicants whose opinion of the United States wasn't negatively affected by years of spurious propaganda spewed out by unfriendly regimes.

For some of the same reasons, Barry Mendelson was enjoying a great deal of success with his recruiting in New Zealand. The foremost expert in matters of taxation lived in

Wellington, New Zealand. He had initiated the Value Added Tax in his country and it had soon spread to Canada and other countries by the start of the 21st century. Ivan and Barry had decided that he should be offered a high-level consulting position to help merge the tax regulations of the two merged U.S.N.A. nations, and supervise the unification and simplification of the tax code. The gentleman in question was retired now, and all that was necessary to get the benefit of his experience was to loosen the work permit arrangements so that he could work in North America.

This was exactly what Ivan Welland's Finders program was meant to accomplish, so when New Zealand's tax expert agreed to come to Washington there was joy in the Federal Department of Personnel, and even Brooklyn had to admit that her husband and her boss had done a good thing for the U.S.N.A. It was unlikely that the man would remain in the U.S.N.A. for the rest of his life because he was a loyal Kiwi, but he realized that he could make a contribution to the most important economy on earth, the one that all others, whether they admitted it or not, depended upon to keep things stable.

How could anyone oppose the gutting of the U.S. tax code, which consisted of 17,000 pages of regulations that practically no one completely understood? Those who saw advantages for themselves in hiding behind the complexities of such a tax code and those who could afford a battery of lawyers and public accountants might have preferred not to tamper with things as they were, but everybody else wanted a fair, simplified flat income tax and competitive corporate taxes. Ivan and Barry had high hopes that their first successful recruit would spur on the North American tax boys to actually do something about the very inefficient, unfair, and unpopular taxation system that was mostly a holdover from the U.S. tax structure.

Mike Dickerson's legal background as a U.S. Attorney was not exactly perfect for recruiting and understanding the work of sub-atomic physicists, but he found comfort in knowing that he would soon be finding candidates who were experts in international law, constitutional law, and maritime law with specific experience from the point of view of European law. In the meantime, however, Ivan had given him a special assignment. He was to survey the physicists at the CERN lab in Geneva to see how many would consider being repatriated to North America. One of the biggest disappointments that Ivan Welland had to endure during his time in the U.S. government was Congress's cancellation of funding for the sub-atomic particle Collider that had been under construction in Texas. Although the costs involved in the project were enormous, and the immediate results to be expected were of importance only to theoretical physicists, Ivan believed that it was of utmost importance to keep control of the doorway to the future of science in the hands of Americans. Allowing the much smaller, less costly European Collider project to go ahead in Geneva was to Ivan's eyes a compromise of major proportions that would shift the balance of physics research to Europe. Welland had discussed this matter with President Quince, and he had been heartened to hear that the new head of the free world would support the reopening of the Texas Collider project.

Abandoning the Collider building project after billions of dollars had been poured into it had resulted in shifting the results of years of scientific research to the European Union. The comparatively pocket-sized Collider now located in the equally pint-sized nation of Switzerland had put limitations on the results that could be achieved. The expected economic boom resulting from the formation of the U.S.N.A. would suffice, in the opinion of both President Henry Quince and Secretary Ivan Welland, to refinance and restart the Texas Collider construction project. Mike Dickerson's recruiting in Europe was considered by them to be a start in the direction of staffing the resurrected project. The wisdom of this was being borne out by the financial crises occurring in most of

Europe, which could very easily result in the discontinuance of the CERN Collider project. When the Higgs-Boson was verifiably discovered in Geneva, however, the situation heated up in more than one way. The Geneva Collider itself was too small to efficiently verify the preliminary findings, and without scientific verification the discovery of the Higgs Boson would remain theoretical. These factors were obvious to the scientists working in Geneva and boded well for Mike Dickerson's efforts to recruit European scientists.

When Dickerson arrived in Europe he didn't know a Boson from a Bison. He had no idea how the physicists were going to prove that it existed. This absence of knowledge sent him scurrying to a number of sources for explanations. One of the sources that he consulted described a Boson as a celebrity sub-atomic particle that goes to a party and is immediately surrounded by other particles wishing to bask in his popularity. When the Boson was at the party he doled out wisdom and was lionized to the extent that he couldn't move to the other side of the room or exit the party. What he doled out appeared in the form of mass, which the other particles absorbed. Doling out mass on even the tiniest imaginable scale was what made certain scientists refer to the Boson particle as the "God Particle." Dickerson didn't know if this explanation was sufficient to make him seem knowledgeable in the conversation with incipient candidates for immigration under the Finders program. Either way he had no choice but to continue in his ignorance, as it was too late for him to become a theoretical physicist himself.

The discovery of enormous oil reserves in the Caspian Sea Basin had provided Russia with unexpected wealth sufficient to finance their own Collider. Dickerson became aware that the Russians were sniffing around the scientists employed by CERN with the aim of possibly staffing their project. The number of doctoral-level sub-atomic physicists in the world was a small club, so the identification of these scientists was not difficult to ascertain. Because the Russian leaders wanted to return their nation to the important place in the world that they had held during the Cold War, building a Collider might be just the thing they needed to restore them to prominence. Cooperating with NASA in doing space launches had already shown how Russian science could be put in the forefront. In fact, many leaders in the world of politics had observed this supposed international cooperation and suspected that it was just a matter of time before Russia supplanted the U.S. as the leading space explorer. From the point of view of cost sharing, cooperation was the best way to offset the enormously expensive frontiers of science, but from a political standpoint the idea of sharing power was anathema, especially to nations with old grudges and very different ideas about governing people.

National rivalries long thought to be dead were, in fact, not dead at all. The emergence of the U.S.N.A. as the largest nation on earth was not good news to many in the Russian hierarchy. Unfulfilled aspirations of world domination by the Soviet Communist regime still burbled beneath the surface of international politics in the Kremlin. Mendacity was still alive and well in the inner circle of Russian government. The KGB that had reigned supreme during the Cold War years was undergoing resurgence. Under its new appellation as the FSB, the old guard was quietly seizing power again.

Boris Yukovich, Olga's father, was now a senior KGB officer whose reputation as a hard-liner was intact. He was resurfacing as a leader of a faction that wanted to control the reinstatement of the old KGB operating philosophy, but until he was absolutely certain of his support, he had to remain quietly behind his desk in the FSB's Foreign Intelligence Service. Boris used his agent daughter operationally to perform tasks that he didn't want to put his stamp on. Olga had more than delivered value for his having found her a job at the FSB—in fact she had become the number one Russian Secret Agent in a particular kind of espionage activity. She was nicknamed the "Assassinator" because of her successful record in the specialized field of international eliminations.

When Boris Yukovich learned about Welland's targeted immigration program, he called Olga into his office.

"Olga, it is seldom that a person with your particular specialty is invited to enter the headquarters of the enemy. I know your falsified curriculum vitae has been passed along to the Americans... I mean to the U.S.N.A. people. And I know you have been invited to a second interview in Washington. Needless to say this is a marvelous opportunity for you to use your talents on behalf of Russia and the Yukovich family. Never since the day when your great grandfather put the ice pick into that cowardly traitor Trotsky, has an opportunity like this arisen. We must take advantage of it."

"You are right, Father. I shall enjoy killing that fool, Ivan Welland."

"Ah, my dear, but I am not thinking of him. You must raise your sights a little."

"You mean, President Quince?"

"Of course, Olga. Did I not train you to go after your opponent's King without mercy?"

"Yes, Father."

"We must carefully put together a plan to take advantage of this opening that has been presented to us. After all, it is the business of our family to excel in this form of political chess game. The sad thing about our vocation is that the better we are at it, the less fame we can expect to get for it."

"That's true, Father, but we two and perhaps a select few will know who are the true chess masters."

"Correct, my child. Now let's get down to the details. It is said that the Devil is in the details, so let's get to work on dispatching that Christian idiot President Quince, who thinks he can edge us out of our place of leadership in the world, and without bloodshed!"

The Yukovich family went right to work planning what is truly the oldest profession in the world. Ever since Cain killed Abel, murder correctly precedes prostitution in the list of Commandments, and it is a more important sin altogether. Olga's mission was to kill both Quince and Welland, if not simultaneously, then one at a time, without a thought about sinning.

Dickerson was enjoying some success convincing the European and the expatriate American physicists at CERN to entertain the idea of coming to the U.S.N.A. to continue their work. Most of them cautiously predicated their favorable response on the project's getting Congressional approval with a sufficient doling out of funds to rebuild what had already been done, and then subsequently abandoned, on the Collider in Texas. Mike Dickerson promised there would be enough money appropriated to permit rehiring and tenuring the project's key physicists. This was necessary since senior candidates in sub-atomic physics were not about to give up their sure-thing employment in Europe to take a flyer on the U.S.N.A.'s promise of a rejuvenated Collider program in North America.

CHAPTER EIGHT

In an effort to save money on transportation, Ivan had arranged for one plane to make several stops and pick up all the candidates in each major city. The charter flight format had the effect of generating a certain collegiality among the passengers. Several were acquainted with each other through memberships in professional societies, while others in the same fields of endeavor were known to each other by their writings and journal articles.

For some of the invitees it was like old home week, but for Olga, who had asked to meet the flight in London, it was a lonesome trip because she, not being a real scientist in the field of computer science, was not familiar with those who would normally have been colleagues. Colonel Cutler had noticed that Olga Yukovich didn't socialize, but he attributed it to gender shyness based on the fact that she was a single, moderately attractive albeit unusually tall female, traveling with a mostly male planeload of elite and highly accomplished citizens of the world.

The chartered flight began in Auckland, New Zealand, where it took on board the country's multi-talented head of the Agriculture Department's ovine laboratory. He was also an eminent tax expert and the botanical whiz who had more or less single-handedly invented the Kiwi fruit. Then, skipping over to Sydney, the plane picked up some experts in various fields such as mining, agriculture, and engineering, all distinguished gentlemen rounded up by Barry Mendelson. Both Barry and Ivan knew that highly successful Anzac candidates would be less likely to leave their countries to become permanent immigrants in the U.S.N.A., so they had created a special category of work permits that let these specialists get green cards and begin working immediately.

The free flight, the opportunity to meet other experts and potential employers and to receive V.I.P. treatment during this introductory interviewing jaunt was hard to refuse. Ivan and representatives from the U.S.N.A. who had shown some interest in meeting these people had offered programs that included tours of facilities, interviews with senior represent-atives, and introductions to leaders whom they might never have met had it not been for Ivan Welland's full court press immigration policy.

Candidates from countries like Russia, the Middle East, and China that were not likely to allow their star citizens to evacuate were handled on an individual basis. Ivan Welland, Cutler, and Mercer had decided that the best way to proceed with nations that restricted the personal foreign travel of their citizens was to examine the records of university students from these nations who had studied in Canada and the U. S. By consulting with professors and their fellow students it was often possible to ascertain which students were the most talented in the disciplines that were needed by the U.S.N.A. economy. Admittedly this was a slower, more intensive way to recruit experts from these countries, but finding the future leaders in vital areas of the economy was so much easier to do this way than by allowing random immigration or quotas to supply the required individuals to meet the needs of the U.S.N.A. Immigration policies that are slow, requiring years of waiting and the filing of documents in translation to sup-port the candidacy of family-sponsored immigrants could not efficiently meet the massive needs of the new U.S.N.A.

Mike Dickerson and his recruits were picked up at Charles de Gaulle airport in Paris. Then it was a short hop to Heathrow Airport in London to board Mary O'Neal and her candidates from the E.U. Byron Begley and his candidates from South and Central America were rounded up in Sao Paulo and flown in a separate charter flight to Dulles Airport. A total of 273 candidates received invitations to interview with interested employers. It had been an enormous job to make the arrangements for housing, feeding, and meetings for this large group of candidates. Ivan had put his trusted assistant Brooklyn in charge of this aspect of the Finders program. After all the candidates had been checked into their hotel rooms, they were given the rest of the day to adjust to jet lag and to the culture shock of being in the U.S.N.A. An orientation session was set for nine o'clock the following morning, and Secretary Ivan Welland was to deliver the welcoming address. The next day at lunchtime, President Quince was scheduled to address the candidates.

Promptly at nine o'clock in the morning Ivan began his orientation. He arose from his seat and tapped the mike a few times before proceeding.

"Good morning, everyone," he began. "My name is Ivan Welland. I'm the Cabinet Secretary for Federal Personnel, and I'd like to welcome you to the United States of North America on behalf of our new Government. I'd particularly like to greet each of you on behalf of our first President, Henry Quince, who will be here to speak to you tomorrow after lunch. You will hear the words *new* and *first* a lot in the course of your time here. Don't be dismayed by this, as we have many centuries of experience in democratic governing in the two nations that have now joined together to form the new United States of North America. The merger of Canada and the United States into one new nation has opened up expansion opportunities of a great magnitude.

"Each of you was invited here to explore these new opportunities with us. My job is to help President Quince to find talented people to fill the positions that have opened up due to the creation of the U.S.N.A. President Henry Quince recognized that the old immigration policy was going to be too slow in producing enough skilled candidates to fill the positions available, so he asked me to design changes in our immigration policy that would meet our requirements.

"The merger of our two countries has created an economic expansion of unprecedented proportions. We could no longer sit back and wait for people such as you to voluntarily enter North America under the existing immigration systems. So I'm happy to announce that I've been asked to go out to find you. This is the first time in history that such a thing has been attempted on this scale, so we are experimenting with another first—something that is altogether new. As we all know, things almost never succeed perfectly the first time they are tried, so I hope you will bear with us as we work the kinks out of our first effort at a targeted immigration policy.

"Over the last decade the combined number of legal immigrants to Canada and the United States have been over 1.4 million people per annum. In addition, it is estimated that the current illegal resident population of North America is a minimum of 11 million adults. You may have heard it said about a country that it is a nice place to visit, but not a great place to live. From these figures you can see that our continent proves the reverse to be true—it is a nice place to visit *and* to live. Over seventy percent of those who immigrate to our continent choose to remain and become citizens. We believe that immigrants come here primarily to share in our prosperity, and they generally stay because they find it.

"The formation of the U.S.N.A., and conditions in the world at large, have not changed the perennial search for freedom and prosperity. What has changed today is the speed at which things move. In order to continue to lead humanity in this search, the new nation of the U.S.N.A. must intensify its efforts to find leaders who are willing to help us expand and grow our economy to prepare for the future. In case you haven't guessed, your presence here is in direct response to that need. So we pledge to make an honest effort to find the best people, to offer them the best opportunities in the world, and to enfold them into our new nation's expansion."

Out in the audience Olga Yukovich, anonymous in the midst of the other candidates, listened to Ivan's speech. She heard what he said, but she thought it was just a clever ruse. Imagine collecting, under the auspices of the President of the

U.S.N.A., the most talented individuals in all the critically important areas of life in one room at the same time with the intention of offering them a better position than the ones they presently held. It was head-hunting audacity carried to the maximum level. She almost felt it *de rigueur* to do what she could to foil his plan, for after all, wasn't that why the FSD had sent her on a mission to Washington?

In spite of Olga's being in full accord with her mission, her thoughts returned to Princeton and the night of her chess match with Ivan Welland and its aftermath. She was seeing Ivan in her mind's eye as he strode around on the stage with the microphone in his hand. Since that night she had plenty of time to recall how this man had thoroughly humiliated her on the chessboard. Her ego had been permanently damaged by that incident, and although she was as bitter as Socrates' cup of poison hemlock, she had none of the great philosopher's humility or quiet wisdom. Instead, she worked unremittingly on her secret plans for revenge.

Ivan continued his speech, aware that Olga was in the audience, but unable to see her in the dimly lit room.

"For the sake of efficiency we've divided you into occupational sectors, using your CVs and matching them to potential employers. The identity cards that you were given show the designations and room numbers where you will go after I conclude my remarks. We'll meet back here at twelve thirty for a drink, followed by lunch at one o'clock. Then there will be more interviews this afternoon. Tonight you're on your own for dinner. Tomorrow at lunchtime President Quince will address you, and after that there will be more interviews culminating in cocktails and a gala dinner in the main dining room at seven o'clock."

Olga Yukovich was convinced that her disappearance would go unnoticed in the confusion of the job market atmosphere taking place after Ivan Welland's speech. She hated the free market system. She believed in an elite central governing group, not in the chaos of a democracy where all the people took it for granted that they had a right to their own opinions. The wisdom of the masses was anathema to her and to her father, who had taught her how to play the game of life. It was unlikely that she would ever be in North America again, so she felt obliged to accomplish what would be her magnum opus. As the others left the assembly room, Olga headed outside in search of a hardware store.

She was right about the confusion that occurred when Ivan's staff was making introductions and directing people to the appropriate interviewing rooms. Olga wasn't missed. She left the hotel by a side door and went straight to Dupont Circle, where she found a neighborhood hardware store that one of the candidates had described to her. It was stocked with at least one of everything that could possibly be found in an old-time hardware store. In terms of organization, none was in evidence. Customers were obliged to speak to the elderly owner if they wanted to find what they were looking for. Olga followed him in his meandering course through the store to locate the items she had listed on a scrap of hotel stationery. The sound of their accents in spoken English—his Yiddish and hers Russian—reverberated off the dusty metal shelving.

Having temporarily appeased the God of Babel, Olga hurried back to her hotel room. Using the technology, or rather the ingenious lack of bomb-making technology that the FSD had learned from its experiences with the Islamic Chechen rebels in the Northern Caucasus, she assembled a small but deadly IED from the elements she had purchased in the hardware store. The flattened device fit inside a slit which she made in the covering of a rubberized floor mat of the kind used by chefs or machine operators. The detonator was an ultra-sound-activated sparker that ignited incendiary chemicals that would set off a small but potent plastic explosive charge. The result would be a white-hot burst of flames followed immediately by an explosion that would flash up the victim's legs, tearing bone and flesh from the bottom up. Olga had worked with the bomb experts at the FSB to develop a signal-producing device hidden in a hearing aid. She would then be able to set off the blast later on by making a small, unobtrusive adjustment to the hearing aid. Survival of such an attack was unlikely. Her expectation was that President Henry Quince would surely die, if not at once, then after suffering excruciating pain.

Her plans for Secretary Ivan Welland were similar as to the intended result, but different in the method of execution. The assassination of her old chessboard vanquisher had to be accompanied by a liberal dose of humiliation. As the world's most successful assassin, albeit the least famous (the ranking of a professional killer is in direct proportion to his or her anonymity), Olga's true talent went unrecognized by the world, since it follows that the best-known murderers are likely to be the least talented in professional competency. Viciousness, hideous creativity, and cold-bloodedness are all attention-getting devices of a criminal mind, but the true assassin must be judged by the ability to get away with the crime. Never since the hey-day of the Jackal had one person dispatched so many political enemies of the State and been so perfectly anonymous as had Olga Yukovich. Her father had taught her well. As a chess player and an international agent, she was unquestionably one of a kind.

Olga's association with the sport of volleyball, first as a player and then as an assistant coach of the Russian national team, had provided her with a cover activity that allowed her to travel the world. She would ostensibly make arrangements to attend international competitions, but in reality she used this occupation as a front to gain entrance to countries whose leaders needed to be brought into line with Russia's policies. Thus Olga's passport was stamped with the official entrance and exit dates that coincided with the demise of many seemingly unrelated political world figures. The FSD, like its predecessor the KGB, preferred the "final solution" method of ridding the field of undesirables. There was something appealing, Olga mused, about the finality of assassination as a solution to resolving problems with those individuals who strayed from the path. It is no wonder that the Russian Mafia adopts similar methods of operation to those used by people in political power. The terror that can be engendered from the bloody assassination of an opposition leader, recalcitrant victim, or competitive adversary can yield results that are unmatched by any peaceful means of conflict resolution.

Over the years Olga had gained an impressive reputation in Russia for being the best in the business of permanently removing those people who stood in the way of the Russian government's plans, but she was also the Kremlin's best-kept secret. Of all the cognoscenti who were privy to the identity of the "Scalpel," as she was called in the FSB, none dared to criticize her as long as her work was carried out with surgical precision.

Her success brought a certain cachet to her father, too. After all, hadn't he trained her? The irony in the references to her surgery was that all her patients inevitably died. In the beginning she had often relied on her father to provide her with advice and support, but as time went by and she gained more confidence, she relied on him less and less. Her father was worried about her growing independence, for he knew from giving her chess lessons that she had a tendency to underestimate her opponents and occasionally to act hastily.

These were not the right characteristics to cultivate in a business such as theirs. Shortly before she left on her journey to Washington he had spoken to her about becoming careless and believing in the dangerous myth of her own infallibility. She had ignored his warnings, thinking he was jealous of her mounting prestige, so she silently gloated about the growing number of ultimate checkmates that she was chalking up.

One of the attributes that made her highly successful was her ability to use her femininity to her best advantage. Her height, however, which was not uncommon for volleyball and basketball players, was a disadvantage when it came to attracting the opposite sex. Being tall called attention to her, and attention, like fame or notoriety, was anathema to a serial murderess. She was unable to play the role of the little woman with any but the tallest men, thus forfeiting a great advantage in interpersonal gender relationships. She was most often treated by men as a freak of nature—an oddity like a giraffe among antelopes or a whale among fish. On the one hand she was proud to tower over most women, but on the other hand she hated having to stand out in a crowd. Eventually she learned to behave like a regal princess when in a group, standing tall and aloof as though she deserved special obeisance from the ranks of the vertically challenged, simply by virtue of having long legs.

With men it was different. Some men seemed to regard her as a challenge. They treated her as though she were a mountain to be climbed. Those who accepted the challenging aspects of Olga were often rewarded, but never with honesty. From her observations she was sure that tall men were the recipients of a great deal of success that was attributable to their height, not their abilities. Surprisingly, shorter men who were undaunted by her height tended to be the wealthiest. Those men whose egos could overcome the challenge of being short without losing their masculine self-confidence were often the most interesting specimens of their gender, but Olga assassinated the short and the tall with impunity. When it came to sexual attractiveness, however, Welland was still at the top of her list. Her analytical, chess-oriented brain could never completely understand why that was the case, even after so many years.

Olga was confident that all would go as she had planned as far as the explosion was concerned. The only possible problem was getting the floor mat placed behind the podium before the speeches began. Security personnel were in evidence during the earlier meeting, and no doubt the room would be scanned carefully by the Secret Service prior to the

President's scheduled appearance. Her only hope of gaining access to the podium seemed to be to obtain Secret Service identification so she could blatantly walk into the hotel's ballroom, overtly place the mat, and leave the room as if she had been assigned to do so.

When she got back to her room she removed a lipstick and a small perfume vial from her cosmetic kit. The barrel of the lipstick container was also the barrel of a hypodermic needle. She charged the needle with the clear liquid in the perfume bottle, then she spritzed a fine test stream into the sink. Convinced that everything was in order with the device that the FSD had christened the "Yukovich," she placed the lipstick in the pocket of her business suit jacket and left the room.

CHAPTER NINE

President Henry Quince was rehearsing his speech by reading it aloud and timing himself. "My esteemed candidates," he began. "Ladies and gentlemen, Doctor Welland, and all the staff members who have worked so hard to put this special program of intensive and targeted immigration into place, I extend our grateful nation's welcome to all of you with the hope that many of you will accept my invitation to join us in the creation of the United States of North America.

"This is not in essence a new idea. Historians estimate that perhaps as few as 400,000 crossed the Atlantic during the 17th and 18th centuries. During this period approximately 175,000 Englishmen migrated to North America. The epochs since then have seen mounting immigration numbers with periods when northern Europeans provided the majority of immigrants, giving way to an influx of Southern and Eastern Europeans, until the present day when the largest number come from Latin America and Asia. Major changes in the world included wars, depressions, and political and religious persecutions, which motivated people from elsewhere to come to America. Canada and the United States in the past received immigrants in three principal component categories: the social, which refers mainly to family reunifications; the humanitarian, which relates essentially to refugees; and the economic, with particular emphasis on the contributors who improved the economy by means of investments or by filling labor market requirements. Our present targeted immigration program is a build-on to the economic component.

"The difference between the present program, of which you are all a part, and the former immigration program, is that you candidates are being *invited* to immigrate. This invitation doesn't come out of necessity, because North America will succeed whether you come to join us or not. Instead, our invitation is extended to you as a synergistic opportunity. We believe we can offer you the greatest chance in the world to advance in your personal endeavors while simultaneously providing our new unified nation with the opportunity to maximize its efforts by injecting and partnering its economy with some of the world's leading minds in science, technology and the humanities.

"Many of you have received invitations from specific organizations that requested my government to ask you to visit their facilities to discuss mutual interests with them. We wish you to have fruitful discussions with these employers, and we hope many of these talks will result in your coming permanently to the U.S.N.A. Arrangements for travel and scheduling will be made for you, which you can obtain from your Finder after this assembly adjourns."

Quince had arrived at this point in his speech when his Chief of Staff interrupted him.

"Mr. President, excuse the interruption, but Secretary Welland is here and he's requesting a brief meeting."

"Very well. Show him in."

"Good day, Mr. President."

"What's on your mind, Ivan?"

"Well, sir, I've been concerned since I suggested the program for targeted immigration that some errant nation might try to use this opportunity to penetrate our security in order to create havoc and bring our synergistic unification plan into disrepute."

"Have you any evidence that this is happening?"

"No solid evidence, but my intuition is on high alert, and I've learned to pay attention to it over the years."

"Over my seventy years of life, Ivan, I've learned that usually the most important things are the controversial ones in which we have little solid evidence for believing."

"I know what you mean, Mr. President."

Quince was, in Ivan's opinion, more of a philosopher than he was a politician. Perhaps that was why Ivan thought he was such a good politician. He assumed POTUS was referring to matters of faith and the mysteries of life that couldn't be solved by a totally rational approach.

"Well then, what is it, Ivan, that makes you suspect that something suspicious is afoot?"

"It has to do with a certain Russian citizen that one of my Finders invited to this conference. I recognized her name on his list of candidates. Years ago this woman was in a graduate program in the Math department at Princeton when I was a student there. I knew her quite well, and I distrusted her then as I do now."

Ivan didn't want to get into the details concerning his acquaintanceship with Olga, but he realized that he would have to speak about more than just his general opinion of her character if he was going to get the President to agree to the extended security measures he intended to recommend.

"And this woman is here now as one of our candidates?"

"She is."

"So what do you suggest that we do about it?"

"Well, for the present we're operating in the shadows. I haven't seen or heard of Olga Yukovich for nearly twenty years, so I can't say with any degree of certainty that she's a menace. It's just a strong feeling I have. I propose that we have our intelligence people investigate her background. She could have become the software developer she claims to be, or she could be using a false résumé to gain entrance to our targeted immigration program."

"Shall I have the C.I.A. do a work-up on her?"

"That might be wise, and if you could alert the Secret Service to keep an eye on her that might also be helpful."

"Consider it done, Ivan."

"Thank you, Mr. President."

In some of his previous posts Ivan Welland would have had a much more direct connection to the services of the various Homeland Security agencies, and he could then have had direct control of the investigation, the surveillance, and the interdiction of perpetrators. Unfortunately his present cabinet post was one step back from his former hands-on security jobs, so now he had to request assistance from the law enforcement side of government rather than order it.

Unfortunately this procedure involved time delays and brought turf protection issues to the fore. Agency directors would use their own judgment as to the priorities to be given to the assignments handed over to them. On top of the usual bureaucratic holdups, the fact that every agency within the newly united country was new at their jobs meant that there would be snafus in getting oversight on Olga's activities.

Good assassins thrive on chaos, great ones create it, and good politicians generate obstacles so that overcoming them can make them famous. President Quince, being a good man, was ill-prepared for political leadership because he nurtured an unrealistic belief in the purity of motivations in others. Ivan Welland knew all this about President Quince, and Olga Yukovich counted on it. Ivan wanted to protect his innocent leader, and Olga wanted to destroy him. Thus the opposing sides were forming up for the battle to come.

Quince unhurriedly looked into his many bureaucratic resources to soothe his Secretary's paranoid fears about his long-time nemesis. Welland recognized the danger of not responding to a threat like this immediately. Even though his present portfolio gave him no authority over security matters, Ivan decided to take a few precautions of his own. The Finders were a cadre of tried-and-true heroes, who like him were presently acting in less dangerous capacities, but if called upon they still retained the experience of a small, potent strike force. So in spite of the busy day that they had ahead of them while shepherding their candidates around the interviewing process, Ivan called them together for a special meeting.

Ivan, whose speeches always revealed the underlying academic in him, began his talk by quoting from Chuang-tzu, circa 300 B.C. "Banish wisdom, discard knowledge, and gangsters will stop!" He then paused for effect, before continuing. "I take issue with this sage of the ages. I prefer the Boy Scout motto, *Be Prepared.* Our enterprise here is a new advancement in democratic liberty. Our objective is to reach out to targeted individuals who can help make the idea of a United States of North America an economic success, but there are those who wish us ill and will do anything to stop us from succeeding. Openly offering to share our new opportunities with talented individuals from other nations has provoked a response in some quarters that is hostile, to put it mildly. In theory it occurred to us that certain violent dissenting elements might try to put a stop to our plan, but we hoped for the best. But have we prepared sufficiently for the worst? I believe we have not.

"Each of you participated with me in various previously successful actions that headed off terrorist attacks. I suspect it is again time for you to suit up and follow your Quixote as he attempts to interdict yet another evil attempt to foil our efforts to pacify and prosper the world we live in. I need you to help me avoid what I suspect is going to be an attempt to publicly embarrass the U.S.N.A. by crashing our program of targeted immigration. Helping to put an end to this endeavor may entail personal danger, so I must inform you that you'll be cooperating in this operation on a purely voluntary basis. I need to know by a show of hands if you are willing to volunteer. You may well ask why, if this is a security matter, we can't leave it to those agencies whose job it is to insure our safety. I can tell you that I have spoken to the President and he has agreed to put the Department of Homeland Security on high alert. So again you may ask why we need to be involved. I fear that because our newly-merged nations are at the early stages of the unification process, we may not yet be able to act quickly enough to thwart a sophisticated terrorist attack. We can't risk lives, and the program's objectives, while we wait for bureaucratic snarls to be worked out. So I'm asking you now to indicate by a show of hands that you are willing to volunteer to do what you can to help."

As soon as he had the unanimous show of hands from his Finders that he hoped for and expected, Ivan launched into the explanation of the plan he had devised to counter the attack that he hoped would never occur.

Olga had spent most of her working life among operatives of the Russian Secret Police. After she retired as a volleyball player she coached on a part-time basis, which had kept her active and fit. These activities were carried out among people who were competitive to a fault. Neither group was bothered much by morals. Their definition of success was victory, and victory would suffice if won fairly or otherwise.

Olga had always found it easy to adapt herself to this environment, for living with her father had been a survival course in competition on every level. The act of spiking the volleyball became a source of great physical satisfaction to her. Check-mating a chess opponent was a mental and an emotional satisfaction of great proportions. But when she discovered the rewards of the assassin's trade, made legitimate by the governmental authority of the FSB, she knew she had found her true métier.

The dissolution of the Soviet communist states and the corrupt political leadership of Gorbachev, Yeltsin, Putin, and Medvedev had seen Russia in a down-spiral that removed them from their superpower status in the world. Russian pride had suffered a great deal when the transition from a communist police state operated by the Politburo became the democratically elected Russian Soviet Federative Socialist Republic in 1991. The politically inexperienced oligarchs who grabbed power during this period suffered from several internal conflicts in Chechnya, Dagestan, and Afghanistan. Total economic collapse was narrowly avoided when the oil conglomerate Gazprom discovered significant reserves of petroleum in the Caspian Sea region. The economic benefits from oil riches began to raise the GDP, and the improving economy placated dissenters enough so that United Russia, the largest political party in the country, could cement its hold on the government. Since then Vladimir Putin, whose background was as head of the Soviet NKVD, and his chief of staff Dmitry Medvedev, who was the Chairman of the Board of Gazprom, ruled the country absolutely in spite of violations of human rights, claims of electoral fraud, and widespread corruption.

Regardless of some outward appearances of democracy in modern Russia, the country continues to be governed by relatively few individuals, whose modus operandi remains unchanged since the days of the Soviets. The continuing gangster mentality of the leaders of Russia can be seen in the growth of the Russian mafia, the bullying policies it employs in the U.N., and its secret programs fostered by the activities of the agents of the FSB such as Olga Yukovich and her father. When Chairman Mao said, "Every communist must grasp the truth: political power grows out of the barrel of a gun," he was speaking the political language that Russians understood, perhaps even better than the Chinese. Olga's truth included not only the gun but also every weapon, actual or psychological, to encourage submission and put the fear of death into the minds of her opponents. Russian roulette was, in her mind, not really Russian at all. Roulette was French. It would be better to call the game Olga played Russian chess, or better yet, Yukovich chess.

Oddly enough, the refinements in the rules of Olga's chess game traced back to her match with Ivan Welland at Princeton. Since the unbearable ignominy of that night she had contorted the rules to include a secret penalty for anyone who defeated her. Fortunately her special rule had been applied only rarely. She was truly a strong player, and was seldom beaten on the board. But because of Olga's desperate desire to avenge any loss, bringing a victorious opponent to his ultimate loss was her remaining source of satisfaction. It was in this way that she discovered her true capacity to turn defeats into victories. Strangely enough it was her loss to Ivan Welland that had magnified and focused her desire for victory—a desire that was born in chess, rose in sports, and blossomed in her successful career with the FSB. She had thought him gone and forgotten in her life, but his Finder program had given her a second chance to avenge her loss, and she couldn't resist this opportunity to enjoy some belated vengeance.

Olga didn't think of herself as a murderer. She saw her assassinations in the light of von Clausewitz, as necessary political acts. She didn't kill randomly, passionately, or for pleasure. She saw herself as an authorized operative of the State. She was licensed to perform pre-emptive strikes upon those who stood in the way of her government's righteous plans. She was highly acclaimed by those who knew her work, and she was well paid for it. Gradually she was given great latitude to decide the specific methods to be used in carrying out her assignments. It was in this phase of her profession that she had developed her greatest creativity. Her job this time was to kill the first President of the U.S.N.A. in a very public way in order to demonstrate that the newest, largest country on earth was vulnerable and was not going to dominate the international scene.

For this particular operation she had designed and built a small but lethal IED from commonly available parts. It would go off with a loud bang while President Quince was giving a public address. The sudden explosion would show the Finders that all the grandiose plans that Quince had made for the U.S.N.A. could be made to vanish in a puff of smoke. Olga was absolutely confident that her plan was foolproof, provided the mat could be put in place on the floor in front of the speaker's podium. All that remained for her to do was to figure out how to situate the explosive device. Just as any professional would have done, she had carefully inspected the premises and decided that she would have to place the mat herself. The staff involved with the production of the event were wearing identification badges with their photos on them. In addition, the maintenance and cleaning staff were wearing uniforms. Security officers were posted here and there around the conference center, so any suspicious activities would likely attract their attention. The question for Olga was whether it was better to try to place the mat in the daytime when the auditorium was abuzz with activity, or do it at night in the off hours when no one was around. She decided on the latter course.

At 10:30 at night Olga took the ice pail from her room and made a trip around the twelfth floor. If anyone spoke to her she would say she was looking for ice to refill the metal bucket. As she rounded a corner she noticed a door that was marked "Employees Only." She opened the door and found it was a small room containing cleaning materials, a supply of clean towels, and a shelf stocked with personal hygiene items. There was also a green plastic bin on wheels with some soiled laundry in it, and another containing restocking items for the guest rooms. In addition there was a vacuum cleaner and some brooms and brushes. In one corner of the room there was a hook which held a maid's uniform. Next to that was a small sink beneath a vanity mirror, no doubt put there so the employees could check their appearance before venturing out into the hall to perform their duties.

Olga left the room and continued inspecting the hallway. She soon discovered an alcove that contained an ice machine and a vending machine with some packages of food items. All in all it was a typical hotel set-up with nothing out of the ordinary about it. When she had finished casing her floor she returned to the service closet, put the maid's uniform on the cart, and wheeled it to a position just outside the door to her room. She opened her door, grabbed the uniform and went inside to put it on. When she was fully satisfied that she looked like a hotel maid, she carefully put the floor mat on the cart and covered it with some towels. She pushed the cart to the employee's elevator and took it down to the conference floor level. When the elevator doors opened she found herself in a well-lit corridor. She pushed the cart along, following signs that led her to the convention auditorium, stopping only to peak in at the ladies' washroom that was just off the speaker's stage.

Hearing only some distant chatter and some employees laughing, Olga entered the main hall. She walked up to the podium in a purposeful, businesslike manner, removed the mat from her cart and placed it on the floor behind the lectern, just as though she had been instructed to do so. She then pushed the cart off the stage and left the same way she had entered. She took the elevator up to the twelfth floor and returned the cart and the uniform to the employee's closet where she had found them.

Moving swiftly and silently she reentered her room, and feeling quite sure that she had not been seen, she quickly undressed and got into bed. She looked at the lighted digital clock and noticed it read 11:15. Unbothered by a troubled conscience, she fell asleep immediately.

CHAPTER TEN

Ivan Welland spread his notes out on the table, cleared his throat, and began to address the Finders at their meeting the next morning.

"To be a professor is a curse," he said. "We spend our whole lives trying to avoid the sin of plagiarism, being sure to give credit to anyone who has had the same or a similar idea to ours, lest we be accused of copying. I am, when all is said and done, a professor, which I'm sure you all know very well by now. That's why I so often use quotations from great thinkers to emphasize my points, and also to have someone important to blame if the ideas don't work out.

"There is nothing more difficult to take in hand, more perilous to conduct, or more uncertain in its success, than to take the lead in the introduction of a new order of things.

"Machiavelli said those words way back in the fifteenth century," Welland continued. "With regard to ideas, I find that everything is to some extent derivative of something said or done by someone else. Pursuing our new program of targeted immigration is perilous. Other nations are not likely to appreciate our efforts to woo the best minds in the world away from them. We have already discussed how the Finder approach to recruiting people can enhance the development of the new U.S.N.A. In our system, as you know very well, the individual is free to decide his own destiny. We are openly presenting opportunities, not kidnapping talented people against their will. Candidates who receive job offers are perfectly at liberty to reject them if they wish to remain in their present situations.

"There are a number of regimes in the world, however, that don't permit their citizens to have such personal discretion over their employment, and these may attempt to block our program by the use of violence, so the purpose of this meeting is to head off any such interference by taking preventive security measures."

Neither Ivan Welland nor the members of the audience had any idea that concurrent with their meeting the most successful assassin in the world was at work.

"Because the combined new nation of the U.S.N.A. is still settling in, we are in a vulnerable position. Our national security systems are as yet untried. At this particular time we may be the target of an imminent terrorist attack. I have made my feelings known to the President's National Security Advisor and the Secretary of Homeland Security, but I'm not convinced that at this early stage of our governmental consolidations they can act expeditiously enough or take sufficient measures to protect the participants in this convention, up to and including the President. As a result I'm going to ask you, my experienced cadre of champions, to be on red alert during this period of the Finders program."

"Boss, what makes you think something's up?"

"Well, Barry, you've been an IRS agent for most of your working life, shouldn't you be the most suspicious one of us all? I'm just putting myself in the place of an enemy, and as such I'm thinking this could be an ideal time to attack us."

"You're right. In the IRS we believed that an audited subject was guilty until he could prove himself innocent, not the other way round. But is this the same kind of situation?"

"Perhaps not on a personal level, but on a political level it might be. For instance, if you were the head of an activist group that hated the idea of a democratic free market world economy, wouldn't you like to have the opportunity to blast this initiative out of existence?"

"Yeah, Barry," Captain Mercer chimed in. "Don't you think a terrorist might be better off attacking a peaceful meeting like this one than to openly challenge us militarily?"

"Sure, John. But do we have more reason to believe that they will pick this venue for an attack over any other?"

"Well, after our collegial experience with Ivan during the pirate attack on the largest cruise ship in the world, I think Mary and I can attest to Ivan's superior anticipatory instincts, and in any case it will do no harm to be prepared."

Byron and Mike, who were also participating in the Finders meeting, nodded in agreement, but neither of them had much experience with face-to-face combat situations.

"Regardless of Colonel Cutler's high opinion of me," Ivan continued, "I'm not a military man, and I can hardly tell one end of an AK-47 from the other."

"True enough," Byron agreed, "but you can mow down BS in a document faster than anyone I've ever known."

"I'll second that," said Mike Dickerson, revealing his background as a prosecutor.

"All right, let's stop buttering up the boss and ask him what evidence he has to indicate that we'll soon be facing a terrorist attack," suggested a Finder in the back row.

"I've spoken in passing with Colonel Craig," Ivan said, "about the fact that one of the candidates on his list is known to me. Her name is Olga Yukovich. I told the Colonel that I knew her in graduate school. We were both math students at Princeton. Anyway, she's here now applying to us as a software engineer. It's possible that she acquired this experience later in Russia, but it also occurred to me that she might have been sent here to perform some sort of undercover mission. It may be that she isn't the only agent of an unfriendly nation that's been sent here to take advantage of our generosity. Our selective *job fair* method of encouraging ambitious applicants to seek positions here may also have influenced other competitive nations to send a spy or two to see what we're up to, and possibly interfere."

"This Russian woman… is she likely to be a terrorist?"

"That I can't say, Barry, but she bears watching. That's why I'm going to organize a Finders' surveillance team to function during the remainder of this affair. Each of you will have a part to play until Yukovich is apprehended."

The special meeting continued. Ivan distributed the assignments during the detailed planning session that ensued, and when the Finders were clear about what was expected, the meeting was adjourned so that they could carry out their tasks.

It was 11:30 when they finally broke up. Ivan had been concerned that the tenor of the meetings between the invited applicants and the potential future employers be kept as free as possible from overt security measures. There were to be no physical searches of attendees, and minimal electronic surveillance devices were to be used. Both President Quince and Ivan wanted the affair to be free from any military presence. The image of the U.S.N.A. they wanted to project was of a modern democracy confident in its future and able to give its citizens a degree of liberty not matched anywhere else in the world.

David Feingold was more than an assistant, more than an amanuensis—he was a powerful thinker in his own right. He was a mathematical statistician who had found his milieu in the field of computer science. David was the Finders' head geek. He produced the logic and the algorithms that opened the way for the creation of computer programs and applications that are taken for granted in the cyber world today. It was his work that provided the statistics that Ivan used to convince the President and the Cabinet to go forward with the targeted immigration policy.

David was Ivan's right hand man. He never minded that Ivan was his boss and attracted all the attention, both critical and flattering. Not being the titular leader freed Feingold to focus on solving practical problems. Unlike Ivan, he did not have to deal with personalities. His role was similar to the navigator on a ship or an airplane as he related to the pilot. Whatever happened, he would reach the same destination at the same time, but without all the distractions and responsibilities that come with being in command.

It was Feingold's work that allowed the Finders to interface and merge the dual government's vast databases. Those with the proper security clearances and personal identification could instantaneously search and retrieve information relative to matters large and small, individual and collective, that were now contained in the human resources databank. Secrecy and privacy restrictions were of no account to the few individuals with access to the government's accumulated and classified information.

David Feingold was the nexus of knowledge. He could manipulate data like no other. For the Finders he was like Google on steroids with top-secret clearance, so when Ivan put the Finders on notice that he suspected a threat to the life of the President and the security of their immigration agenda, David went right to work. Like a great orchestra conductor, he coaxed the maximum performance out of his array of electronic instruments. He worked through the night, interfacing the information contained in the databanks of the linked law enforcement agencies throughout the world. In the morning he was able to produce a report for Ivan that, if not evidence, was at least an indication of a possible plot against the life of the President.

President Quince's concept that prosperity was the root motivator for generating immigration was about to be tested. It was admittedly a wild idea to attempt to give the North American economy a shot in the arm by aggregating almost three hundred of the world's leading experts into one room and offering them better jobs. Would personal aggrandizement come before other considerations, or would patriotism, family ties, or cultural traditions be more binding? Faced with the tempting benefits of high salaries, great respect from occupational colleagues and an improved chance of success, would a majority of these candidates forego old loyalties or murderous terror assignments for the opportunity to participate in President Quince's North American sociological experiment?

Ivan had read David Feingold's report. As usual, it was a brilliant summary of the probabilities and possibilities that a dangerous situation might arise, and what the source of the threat would likely be. He devised a plan to counteract a threat by Olga Yukovich that would include his personal intervention.

Everyone would go into the auditorium after breakfast to hear the President's speech. He would attempt to convince them to look favorably upon their forthcoming offers. After that the invitees would meet with their potential employers and colleagues. Many would be taken to locales in which they would work and live if they agreed to accept the offers of employment. Finders and escorts from interested organizations would host candidates and guide them as they sorted through the complexities of the job fair. By the end of the day the Finders would start tabulating the number of new special employment visas that would be issued. At least that was the plan.

At 7:30 the next morning the dining room was already abuzz with excited conversations emanating from the crowd of diverse people who had gathered there for breakfast. The candidates had arranged themselves into small groups based on their national ethnicities or similar occupational relationships, and sometimes both. Ivan arrived and tried to find an empty seat. He regarded with suspicion the fact that the closest available seat happened to be next to Olga Yukovich, but he sat down anyway.

Ivan Welland and Olga Yukovich were probably the least connected to any group or nationality in the room. It had occurred to each of them that the probability of their meeting again after such a long a time was very unlikely, but to others seated at the table their meeting seemed perfectly normal. Nobody knew that an old rivalry between Ivan and Olga had now been restored as though no time had passed.

In the intervening years, Ivan and Olga had achieved a good measure of success. Ivan's had been accompanied by a degree of international fame, while Olga's notoriety was known only to a handful of Russian cognoscenti who had been privy to the results of her secret missions. Nevertheless life had provided each with enough success to give them more self-confidence than they had had in their Princeton days, but the way they dealt with their success was still the same. Ivan had the subtlety to appear guileless, while Olga was openly arrogant and aggressive. An observer who knew them even slightly would have found it strange that Ivan, on his own home ground and with many well-known accomplishments, should nevertheless be guarded and reticent, while this unknown female should be so pushy. The conflict between them flared up again instantly, and as it had been on the chessboard, Olga was full of feints and bluffs while Ivan, seemingly ingenuous, waited patiently in ambush.

"May I join you, Madame Yukovich?" Ivan asked her, as though they had never met. Had she been more alert, she would have noticed that she had been lowered in rank since their last meeting twenty years ago.

"Of course you may join me, Mr. Secretary."

Ivan noticed that she had lost much of her strong accent in the intervening time. She must have been spending a good deal of time speaking English with foreign diplomats.

"How are you enjoying the conference?" he asked her.

"Well, it's an original idea of your President to steal so many smart people all at the one time."

"We are not stealing them. No one is being kidnapped. All the candidates here are completely free to accept or reject any offers they get."

"Well, we'll see how many big fish you catch with your cash bait."

"Cash is not the only bait we're using. Some people like the idea of developing their talents and enjoying the freedom to do so. Why are you here if not for the cash or freedom?"

Feeling as though he had tripped her up, Olga tried to make light of his question.

"I came to see my old friend and fellow alumnus." Her flirtatious expression could not be misinterpreted. "I thought perhaps you would visit me last night for the sake of our old times together."

Ivan received this comment in silence, but it was clear that she remembered their last encounter. "So why did you bother to sign up for this job fair?"

"Well, I think is good idea to see old friend and maybe take job in U.S.N.A. for little while." Olga thought Ivan was behaving just about the way she expected he would. She enjoyed his discomfort with her innuendoes.

Ivan saw that Olga's attitude toward things in general, and to him in particular, had not changed. Physically some bird's feet lines around her steely blue eyes and a small wrinkle or two at the neck were all that he could detect as a result of the inevitable ravages of time. Olga now wore a hearing aid in her left ear, something he didn't remember, but otherwise she looked essentially the same as ever. There was no obvious evidence that his old chess opponent was now a dangerous threat to the security of those connected with, or present at, the job fair. Nevertheless, Ivan felt he should stay close to her and keep a strict eye on her.

"Tell me, Olga, what has life been like for you since you left Princeton? I see you've applied your math skills to the computer field."

"Yes, and also to petroleum engineering problems that lend themselves to computer solutions."

"And how about your personal life? Are you married?"

"No. I am independent person. I don't want hanging-on husband. I suppose you are married, yes?"

"Yes, and I have a daughter, too. My wife, Marina, was Russian, and now she's a citizen of the U.S.N.A."

Ivan said this as if to encourage Olga and to show her that it was possible for a Russian to leave Mother Russia and join the new nation. He also wanted to prove that he was not prejudiced against Russian women. In reality, however, he hoped that she would decline the invitation to relocate to North America if one were extended.

Olga pretended to take this news good-naturedly, but she also couldn't resist injecting a bit of sarcasm.

"Why you tell me this, Ivan? You want me to be jealous of your Russian wife? You want me to feel hurt that you did not ask me to marry you instead?"

Ivan felt uncomfortable with her flirtatious attitude, as though their friendship during their Princeton days had been considerably more than it actually was. There was nothing for it but to play along lightheartedly with her lead.

"But Olga, you were always so independent. How could I have guessed that if I'd asked you, you would have agreed to marry me?"

The truth was that after all the intervening years and his various life experiences, Ivan had come to understand the Christian teaching that sex was permissible only within the bounds of marriage. Every other kind of sex brought with it various aspects of human misery. It was immature to be unable or unwilling to control one's sexual desires, and it was disrespectful to the other person to encourage them to participate. Ivan had noticed that sex outside marriage almost always resulted in unhappiness. He concluded that raising the moral level of civilization would be impossible if our species continued to glorify illicit sex. Passion and excitement might make good theater, but it doomed real life practitioners to addiction. For Olga, however, as in the case of many modern people, it appeared that the situation was quite the reverse. Her interest in sex was entirely selfish. It was composed of three parts power struggle and one part physical gratification.

"I never wanted to marry you or any other man," Olga said, in answer to his question. She was beginning to realize that her flirtatious comments were having the opposite effect from the one intended. Keeping the banter light when talking with the man she wanted to destroy was difficult for her.

Fortunately, other people at the table were anxious to speak to Ivan, and the general breakfast chatter relieved her of having to discuss any more personal details. Eventually she excused herself, claiming that she wanted to return to her room for a little while before the President's speech began.

CHAPTER ELEVEN

I van got up from his seat a few minutes after Olga left the Finders' meeting. He had assigned himself the duty of watching her until she left the country, and he wondered how she would react to this sudden increase of attention. Of all the Finders, Ivan felt he had the best chance of keeping Olga from doing any damage. He had assigned Mary O'Neal the job of secretly searching Olga's luggage while she was at breakfast.

Mary had borrowed a maid's uniform and a passkey and carefully searched Olga's things, but had found nothing noteworthy. Then she joined Barry to monitor the hall security camera to detect any suspicious activity in the hall. They watched Olga enter her room and noted the time. Dickerson, Begley and Captain Mercer were to take up positions around the auditorium and watch carefully for anyone behaving in an abnormal fashion during the speeches. Ivan had to be out of the communications link because he was going to be right next to the primary suspect, and he didn't want to arouse Olga's suspicions.

Once in her room, Olga began her final preparations. She checked her purse to make sure her lipstick was in a handy place. As far as the hearing aid was concerned, she found it annoyingly uncomfortable. She switched it to her right ear, hoping the change would make it less irritating. She stared at herself in the mirror for a minute. One could almost expect to hear the mirror tell her that she was the fairest of them all, which she may have been if all the rest of the Finders candidates had been assassins too.

Just then there was a knock at the door. Olga peered cautiously through the peephole to see who was there, and found herself looking at Ivan's necktie.

"What can I do for you, Ivan?" she inquired, opening the door.

"The conference doesn't start for an hour, so I thought I'd come up for a private visit to catch up on things."

"What things you want to catch?"

Ivan was really only interested in keeping a close eye on his old opponent, but he couldn't get Congreve's famous lines out of his literary mind.

"Heaven has no rage like love to hatred turned, nor hell a fury like a woman scorned," he said to himself, looking at her thoughtfully. He didn't believe for a minute that Olga had ever loved him, but he thought correctly that he had certainly scorned her in the worst way possible when he had shown her no mercy at their games of chess at Princeton. Ivan believed that if he offered Olga a chance to regain her self-esteem by letting her believe that victory could still be snatched from their earlier encounter, she might be deterred or delayed in performing whatever mischief she might be up to. The role of male Mata Hari was foreign to him, but if it had a chance of working, he simply had to try it.

"Olga, I think I was unkind to you when we spoke at breakfast. I guess I was still treating you as a competitor, but there's no need of that anymore, is there? A lot of water has flowed under the bridge. Do you think we could respect each other now, instead of remaining opponents?"

Olga was taken off guard by his attitude. She intended to kill him if she got the chance, although her primary mission target was the President. Logically a double kill of two of the enemy's top officials would only contribute to her legendary reputation at home. She took his softening attitude as a sign of weakness that would play into her hands. Why not have a little fun with this big baby, and sweeten the bad taste she had in her mouth before she disposed of him? She sat on the corner of the bed across from an armchair, and gestured to Ivan to take a seat.

"So you remember me, Ivan, even after so long time?"

"Yes, I remember you very clearly."

Ivan thought if he could keep Olga busy in her room she would not be able to go down to the auditorium to create the mayhem she might be planning, although he didn't know for certain what, or even if, she actually intended to do any harm. He laughed inwardly as he recalled how many women throughout the course of history had used flirtation and sex for political advantage. Maybe he could turn the tables and use sex as a means of distracting Olga temporarily from her murderous goal. The things he would do for his country never included "un-scorning" this woman, but it was a small thing if it saved lives and kept the President safe.

"Tell me what you remember from that time over there," Olga said.

"Okay. I remember we went to your dorm room after the chess match. I remember you gave me vodka."

"What else you remember?"

"I remember how you tricked me into getting me to take off my clothes."

"You think that was trick?"

"Well, maybe not a big one."

Ivan wanted to make Olga think that her seduction of him was a pleasant, long-term memory for him. He wanted to convince her that he really desired her then, and again now, but that the situation had changed. He was married to Marina now, and his former desire for Olga had long since disappeared. Could there be a legitimate excuse for adultery? If the adultery saved many lives, would that legitimize it?

"Tell me Olga, what do you remember of that day when we were together in Princeton?"

Olga remembered every detail of that day, but she was not so dense that she didn't know that she had been the vamp who had ended up being seduced. Her inner conflict was that she had come out of the experience satisfied, whereas if she had had her way she would ironically not have been fulfilled.

"I remember that you were shy to expose yourself. I remember that I let you be on top."

Olga didn't want Ivan to think it was particularly special for her, but the passage of time had not dimmed her memory. When Ivan brought up the subject it had only clarified her recollection, and she felt the stirrings that her memory and his presence provoked once again. This time, however, she resolved to be in charge and stay in charge. Now she was no longer a student driven by unruly emotions. That stage of her life was over. In Olga's mind she was now in total control of her body, and not the other way round. She visualized herself as the master of an arcane discipline that put her in the rarified company of women like Jael, the Hebrew mentioned in the Bible who assassinated the Kenite General Sisera by driving a tent peg into his head.

Olga was wearing a knee-length blue silk print dress that flattered her and served to make her appear feminine. It was one of her standard techniques to make her victims believe that she was far too gentle to be a threat. As she sat on the bed facing Ivan while they talked, she leaned back on her elbows and allowed her skirt to gradually rise up her thighs, giving him an occasional view of her panties as she crossed and uncrossed her long legs. Her knees were at Ivan's eye-level as he sat in the armchair across from her.

Ivan was totally aware of Olga's well-practiced talent in using her sexuality to get what she wanted. He remembered very well her obvious display of cleavage each time she had leaned forward to make a move during their chess match that day in Princeton. The décolleté of the gown she was wearing on that occasion was designed to distract his concentration on the game. Now she was at it again.

The soft outfit she wore on the morning of the Finders' meeting was designed to convey the notion that she was far too ladylike to brutally murder anybody. Although she was in her forties now, she was still attractive enough to pass for someone younger. The way the silk dress was clinging to her emphasized her fit, slender body. Her demeanor was, as usual, totally confident, as if she could have any man she wished. She looked down on men for desiring her. She was suspicious of their motives, and used their hormone-driven nature against them.

Ivan was the one exception that proved the rule. Under different circumstances Olga might have loved him, but as things were, she could only have him for a short time, as she had that time in Princeton. That triumph wasn't long enough to suit her. She wanted no one else to have him, and since that was no longer possible, she was left with only one alternative—use him, enjoy him, and throw him away when she was finished with him.

Olga made up her mind to take Ivan's life in order to avenge the various frustrations she had suffered at his hands. She believed his murder would also further her reputation with the powers at home in Russia. If one assassination were ordered, wouldn't a second be like icing on the cake?

Now here was her chance. They were alone. She knew exactly how she would do it—after all, she had had years to plan it. First, she must get him to undress; that way his body would be found later in a most embarrassing position. If she hurried she could do the deed, leave the body for the maid to find, and still get down to the auditorium in time to take care of President Quince. The most difficult part of the operation, the placement of the bomb, had already been accomplished. All that remained was for her to be in the audience and send the signal to detonate the bomb by pushing the button on her hearing aid.

Ivan realized that if he was going to detain her until after the President spoke, he would have to find a way to keep her in her room. One possible way to do this was to have sex with her again, but this time it would be even more distasteful to him because he was happily married now. He intuited her scheme, but short of killing or kidnapping her when she might possibly be innocent, he had only one way of keeping her voluntarily in her room during the speech. But would it work? She was certainly too much of a professional in everything she did to allow herself to be delayed by a sexual interlude with him, but he could think of nothing else that would serve as a better distraction.

Mary's appointment as a Finder had brought her back into contact with Captain John Mercer. Then their assignments overseas had separated them yet again, but here they were back together once more in Washington, D.C. There was a subtle, magnetic attraction between them, and it was working to prevent them from being drawn apart yet again. They were at that awkward moment when two people separately have stirrings of emotional attachment, but each was wondering if the other was having similar feelings. There were many hints, of course, but action-oriented naval officers were not satisfied with a platonic or unrequited relationship. They had to know clearly the extent of their involvement, so they had both resolved to encourage the development of whatever it was they had. The spark between them had fused, and the gap had closed when John had taken her hand in the elevator after their late meeting with Ivan. Conveniently, but not accidentally, they had been booked into adjoining rooms at Ivan's request. Ivan made for a very tall Cupid, but he just couldn't resist giving propinquity an assist. How often in history had two shy lovers been gently pushed together by the behind-the-scenes machinations of a concerned friend?

After walking hand-in-hand down the corridor from the elevator, they had arrived in front of the door to Mary's room. They were just saying goodnight when John suddenly put his arms around Mary and kissed her. She had returned his kiss, and when she took her hand off the doorknob to put it on the back of his neck, the door had swung slowly open as if the room itself were inviting the couple to go inside. They had stumbled into the room together, and John had pushed the door closed as their kisses grew more passionate.

John drew her tightly up against him so she could feel his desire and unmistakably know his intentions. There followed the usual procession of frantic disrobing until they had fallen on the bed and consummated their long-developing relationship. There was not much sleeping done in Mary's room that night. Nevertheless, by 0700 they were tired but on duty at their assigned posts.

By 7:05 a.m. the President's Secret Service bodyguards had gone over the venue for the speech and hadn't found anything suspicious. Ivan's Finders were posted as had been previously agreed. Commander Mary O'Neal's attention was fixed on the monitor that scanned the corridor on both sides of the door to Olga Yukovich's room.

Barry Mendelson was sitting at the console next to Mary and having the time of his life. He had never been on surveillance before. Barry had, prior to his present assignment, been involved in the sedentary auditing of tax returns for the IRS. He thought his wife should be proud of his being chosen to team up with two Navy Seals and be a Finder, but since Brooklyn was Ivan's Assistant Director she didn't approve of her husband's becoming involved in one of Ivan's often dangerous operations. Barry wisely decided not to call her to tell her what he was up to, even though she had clearance to receive such information.

It was 8:15 a.m. when Barry and Mary had observed Olga Yukovich entering her room. Fifteen minutes later they noted on the screen that Ivan Welland knocked on her door and was subsequently admitted to the room. Ivan had warned them that if they saw Olga come out of the room without him, they should enter the room using the passkey, and see if he was all right.

Under no circumstances was Olga to be allowed to enter the auditorium while the President was speaking. Barry and Mary had evolved a contingency plan that went like this: if Olga left her room alone, before or during the President's speech, they would stop her from getting on the elevator. If no one came out of the room by the time the President had left the building, Mary O'Neal would enter the room wearing the maid's outfit, using some housekeeping pretense if necessary, then size up the situation and liberate Welland. Barry would remain close by and call in reinforcements if necessary.

Meanwhile, inside Olga's room, and particularly inside the heads of its occupants, a deadly version of cold war politics was being acted out. To a neutral observer it might have seemed like glasnost had finally reached its zenith with the two sides preparing for a long-sought accord. In actuality this concurrence was the prelude to a final deadly chess match of conspiracy. Ivan's version of the ending was that his opponent would be prevented from executing her plan and would return home, if not in disgrace, then at least a wiser loser, with no harm done. Olga's concept was that Ivan should be made to pay with his life for thinking that he was her match on a chessboard, in bed, or in his loyalty to his country. Dispatching this idealistic dreamer's President would also be a justifiable political checkmate.

Ivan's preferred tactic called for sweetness and gentleness. He wanted to confuse her with kindness, and make her believe that there was some real affection in their relationship. Alternatively, knowing Olga's nature, he thought he would be more successful if he played his role a bit more passionately, as though he were harboring pent-up desires that had bubbled under the surface for all the years since their last encounter.

Whichever tactic he employed it would be a lie, but he had to be convincing to the same extent as he was convinced that this liaison was necessary for the very best of causes. At any rate, he must keep her busy for the next hour or so. If his plan succeeded she would never know his true feelings, nor would she be conscious of the passage of time until it was too late for her to succeed in executing her own plan. He may have been more innocent than he should have been, but he never thought his own life might be in danger.

Olga's undertaking was to even the score by diverting him. She would pretend to have carried the torch for him for years. She would let him make love to her, and while his attention was distracted, she would kill him quickly by an injection of poison so she could then go on to her principal victim. Her revenge would leave the big American fool's reputation damaged beyond repair. If she succeeded, most likely a hotel maid would discover him naked in the most embarrassing position possible. It would be assumed that he was extracting sex from a grateful Russian woman as a price for having invited her to apply for a job in the U.S.N.A. Until an autopsy could be performed it would be thought that he died of a heart attack in the throes of passion. Olga would simply stick to that story in the unlikely event that she was questioned. Her intention was to leave the country as soon as the bomb went off under the feet of President Quince. She was booked on the first flight to Moscow late that afternoon. There would be no apparent connection between the two deaths, or any proof that she was involved.

Once in her room, Ivan began to speak to her in Russian, hoping to soften her up. Olga replied in kind because it was easier for her to function in her own language. He had almost forgotten how chess-minded she was, and how she always preferred to play the white pieces and make the first move. He took her face in his hands, feeling her ears to see if the hearing aid was still in place.

It was, in fact, still in place, but Ivan was surprised to discover that it was now in the other ear. He had never heard of anyone switching a hearing aid from one ear to the other. Ever alert to details, he reasoned that the device might not be a bona fide hearing aid at all. He wondered if Olga could have had the device adapted to create an electronic detonation signal. His speculations put him on red alert, and helped him to deflect his attention away from the plans that Olga was obviously intending to initiate in the privacy of her hotel room.

Meanwhile Olga was thinking that the fascinating thing about Ivan was that he was more challenging than other men. He didn't relinquish control easily. Vanquishing him would be something like defeating an international chess master in a championship match. It would be difficult, but extremely satisfying. She would have to seduce him quickly and get it over with, though, or she might be late for the President's speech.

"On second thought," she said to herself, "I can take my time about this. It doesn't matter if I kill President Quince at the start or at the finish of his speech. Either way, he will end up being just as dead."

CHAPTER TWELVE

In the hall outside Olga's room there was a steady flow of candidates heading toward the elevator to go down to hear the President speak. Barry and Mary watched their screen intently, but saw no sign of either Olga or Ivan.

"I'm going to take a quick look at Olga's room to see if she's there," Mary said to Barry as she peered at the screen.

"We can't scan the room," Barry reminded her. "It contravenes the privacy code of the U.S.N.A."

"I know, I know. I'll go there personally and listen at the door. Ivan might be in danger."

"Do you want me to come along, too?"

"No, you stay here by the monitor. Contact me right away if you see either of them on your screen."

Mary, still dressed in her maid's uniform and carrying a pistol strapped to her thigh, hurried along the hall in the direction of Olga's room. She had the hotel passkey in one hand and a can of mace in the other. When she put her ear to the door, she heard grunting and scuffling noises, including the crash of something falling on the floor.

Mary put the plastic cardkey in the lock, saw the little green light, and pushed the door open.

"Housekeeping!" she called out as she entered the room.

There in front of her, struggling together like two trained wrestlers, Ivan had Olga were locked in a half nelson. A chessboard was on the floor by their feet, with the pieces spread out everywhere. Just then Olga managed to put her foot behind Ivan's foot and put the full weight of her body against his, forcing him to fall to the floor. She reached over to the bedside table and grabbed her purse, removing a tube of lipstick, which she tried to jab into Ivan's carotid artery, but Ivan blocked her hand. As they wrestled on the bed, the syringe concealed in the lipstick protruded dangerously. If Olga had been able to stick it into Ivan's neck he would have been dead nearly instantaneously.

Mary O'Neal approached the couple and sprayed Olga's face with Mace until she let go of the object in her hand and fell from the bed to the floor. Ivan grabbed the lipstick, being very careful of the hypodermic needle protruding from it. He put the lipstick on the desk across the room, and glanced at Olga's body on the floor.

"I'm glad you got here when you did, Mary. She nearly jammed that needle into me."

"I don't have any restraints to keep her under control."

"Not part of the maid's uniform, I should imagine."

"I do have a peacemaker, however," she said, displaying the pistol she had whipped out of its holster.

"Good. Keep it trained on her, Mary, and be careful. She is the Devil incarnate when it comes to tricks. Call down to John Mercer and tell him to quietly and quickly come here with a pair of handcuffs. I'm going to get dressed now."

Mary got on her radio and did as Ivan instructed. She kept her gun pointed at Olga, who was red faced, teary eyed, and generally miserable. She made no effort to get away or continue the fight. Just then John Mercer arrived at the door.

"John, this is Miss Yukovich," Ivan said. "She's had a little make-up failure, as you can see. She needs to dress and pack. She's taking the evening flight back to Moscow today. I'd like you and Mary to see to it that she looks as normal as possible when you take her to the airport. Take some photos of her, and then get her dressed. Can you do that for me?"

"Yes, sir."

"How did the President's speech go? Were there any problems, incidents, or complications?"

"No, everything went just fine. It was a good speech."

"Very well, then we've done our job."

"Yes, sir."

"We're not through yet, though."

Ivan picked up the lipstick from the desk and showed it to Mercer. "This should be examined by the Secret Service Forensic laboratory. I'm sure the needle contains a lethal dose of a very deadly substance to be determined later. Do not allow anyone to accidentally stick themselves with it."

"Aye, aye sir."

Ivan went to the bed and reached under the mattress. He extracted a device that looked like a hearing aid, and showed it to Mary and John.

"What is that, sir?"

"I suspect it's a detonator. If you look carefully, there's a button that could set off a bomb that needs to be located immediately. You two are busy with this customer, so I'm going to ask Colonel Cutler to get the bomb squad to quietly find the I.E.D. In the meantime if Miss Yukovich is willing to give you its location or any other information about her mission here, which I suspect was to kill President Quince, that could be helpful, but I doubt she'll admit to that."

"May I ask, sir, why are we releasing her? Shouldn't we be taking her prisoner and prosecuting her?"

"No, Captain. If this incident went public it would harm our targeted immigration program. Nobody would want to accept our invitation to come here and work if they thought they were going to be caught up in a terrorist attack. So for the greater good we'll have to ship her back where she came from. This way she can serve as a warning to her superiors that we're vigilant and we won't stand for any aggression."

"Were you playing chess with the captive, sir?" Mercer asked, looking at the chess pieces on the floor.

"I was, John. I had the pleasure of beating this lady at chess when we were students at Princeton, and she was kind enough to allow me to repeat my success here in Washington D.C. Fortunately for the President, Miss Yukovich was so determined to beat me at her national game that she didn't notice how fast the hands of the clock were turning."

"That seems to be a common problem for chess players, sir," Mercer observed. "It's an extremely absorbing game." "Especially when you have a super-strong ego," Ivan agreed, giving Olga a friendly pat on the shoulder. Olga jerked her shoulder away from him as Mercer led her from the room.

Olga sat disconsolately between two Secret Service Agents, waiting for her flight to board its passengers to Moscow. Her mission to assassinate the North American President had failed, as had her effort to rid herself of the memories of her infuriating defeats at the hands of Ivan Welland. Her mind was busy concocting a cover story to rationalize her failure to her father and his cohorts at the FSB. As she turned things over in her mind she realized that it could have gone a lot worse for her if it had not been for Ivan. He could have charged her with any number of serious crimes, including attempted murder, conspiracy to kill a government official, immigration fraud, and others too numerous to list, but all he did was pack her off to Russia. When the time came for her flight to leave she was accompanied to her aisle seat by two guards who stayed with her until the last minute when the doors were sealed prior to take off. The big jet roared down the runway, lifted into the sky, and was soon invisible from the ground as it disappeared into the cloud cover.

The Finders familiar with the circumstances wondered why Olga had been released. In fact, so did Ivan Welland, but he was a cabinet member and he was obligated to think of the larger picture. If it were ever brought to light that the Russian government had sponsored an effort to assassinate the President of the U.S.N.A., the international complications could be horrendous, so he decided to say nothing to anybody. One of the unspoken international understandings was that even with the end of the Cold War the espionage activities between East and West were continuing unabated. It was probably sufficient to send Olga home, where her superiors would surely know of her failed mission. Perhaps this would be a favor to Olga, if it got her name off the preferred list of available assassins. In any case, getting Olga out of the country and out of his hair was a very good thing in itself.

Ivan was disappointed to hear that Colonel Cutler and the bomb squad had not found a bomb. When a visual search failed to turn up anything suspicious, a sniffer dog was brought to the hotel. Even the canine collaborator's olfactory skills failed to discover Olga's IED because she had not used the standard ingredients that the dog was trained to detect. There was one sure way to find the bomb, and that was to detonate it by depressing the button on the hearing aid. That, however, was not an option inside the hotel. The experts finally concluded that the threat must have been only a ruse, and they discontinued the search.

The problem was solved that evening when a hotel maintenance man picked up the rubber floor mat that lay behind the lectern and casually tossed it on a cart, whereupon it promptly exploded. The bomb was a shaped charge of small magnitude designed to send an explosive flash of fiery violence up the legs of the victim standing on the mat. The damage was meant to be localized, and if not immediately fatal to the injured party, it would cause serious wounds which would be painful and slow to heal. As a result of its design the explosion caused by the handling of the mat was startling but not great in a room with a high ceiling like the one in the auditorium. The maintenance man suffered only a few minor injuries from the explosion, and the resulting fire was quickly extinguished. Ivan put the lid on the incident, and the public never knew that they had come within an inch of losing their popular President.

The Finders involved knew just how close the President had come to being killed. Ivan, however, was the only one who understood the situation completely. He had delayed the killer long enough to avert the catastrophe. Had the assassin been anyone other than Olga Yukovich, he might not have been successful in saving the life of the President.

Ivan couldn't help reflecting on how strange life is. He was sure that many times in human history ego had been the tool of choice in affecting the course of politics, but he never would have guessed that a chess game could have held such importance to the world. He would never forget Olga's red-faced concentration and her intense expression as she had struggled to defend her pride and her self-image. Hell, Ivan mused, apparently has no fury like a conceited, egomaniacal, narcissistic woman who loses at chess. Not only had she lost all sense of time while she was engaged in the battle with him, but when she had thrown the chess board along with all its chess pieces in his face, she had forever lost his respect and friendship.

Now that Olga was out of his hair, Ivan was free to assess the validity of his targeted immigration program. He asked his assistant, Brooklyn, to contact those involved and tabulate the results. As a sop to her because she had opposed his making her husband one of his Finders, he assigned Barry to work alongside his wife to do a cost effectiveness study of the program. Ivan hoped this would help Brooklyn to forgive him for sending Barry overseas to do his assignment. He was eager to make a progress report to the President as soon as possible, and he wanted it to be as thorough as possible.

Next, he asked David Feingold to whip up a computer analysis and a printed format for the report. They had started with 273 candidates to fill high-level positions with organizations in various parts of North America. Ivan's department needed to know how many of the invitees had been offered positions and how many had accepted. He also wanted to know how much his recruiting program was going to end up costing. Transportation, hotels, and meal expenses for the interviewing process of 273 candidates were of considerable significance. Would the effort prove worthwhile? That was what Ivan wanted to know, and Barry was the ideal person to conduct the audit.

Aside from the statistical and accounting aspects of the program evaluation, there were all the arrangements that had to be made. Each foreigner that accepted a position had to be shepherded through the immigration formalities. Although the State Department promised to give preferential treatment to Ivan's candidates, there was still much work to be done to arrange visas and security clearances. Ivan assigned his two best lawyers to handle the processing of immigration documents: Brian Begley (with his experience with the F.B.I. in handling security matters) and Mike Dickerson (with his experience as a U.S. Attorney).

Mary O'Neal and John Mercer were assigned the task of coordinating logistics for moving the accepted candidates to the U.S.N.A. Ivan kept Colonel Cutler out of the mix so he could handle special assignments for him, the first of which was to alert all the ICE border entry points to blacklist and prevent Olga Yukovich from ever entering the country again. The second phase of the experimental program involved processing all the immigrants who had been recruited and had accepted employment offers. Ivan wanted them put on the path to U.S.N.A. citizenship as quickly as possible. He realized that this part of the review process could not be completed accurately until the new arrivals had been in the country for some time so that their performance could be compared with that of the unsolicited routine immigrants who had flowed into the country under the old immigration regulations. Evaluating the contributions of individuals to the U.S.N.A.'s economy was going to be a sensitive business, but one that had to be done. Welland had tried to determine what jobs needed filling most urgently. His recruitment had primarily been targeted to occupations in short supply, but considerable effort had been expended to acknowledge the most advanced scientific and technical competencies.

Judging people has always been considered a skill that

requires special talent and insight. The austere black robes of judges are a tip-off that their job is serious and worthy of respect, but judging the value of people to their society is not usually a legal matter for the courts to decide. Everybody makes evaluations of other people's competence. We have evolved tests to help us make judgments, but even these are under constant review. Ivan's objective was to develop a system whereby people could be evaluated from the point of view of their potential value as citizens—job performance being only one aspect of a person's worth to the community.

Ivan was seeking a solution to the question that has puzzled governments since the beginning of time: How can a citizen peacefully consent to be governed by others whose fallibility is all too obvious?

During the ten years of President Quince's tenure in office, the U.S.N.A. saw improvements in nearly every aspect of democratic government. A new era of optimism was born. Economic growth was off the charts. Entrepreneurs were springing up from segments of the population that had formerly been written off. Henry Quince had encouraged the formation of civic research centers that could create experimental microcosms of government functions that needed improvement.

Among these the Center for Election Reform, the Center for Immigration Reform, the Center for Business Ethics, the Centre for Monetary Reform, were but a few. These centers were composed of leading figures in each of the fields to be studied. Experimental mini-government departments were created to test the efficacy of new recommendations for improving the efficient functioning of the new government. No limitations were put on the members of the Centers, except that their considerations had to be free of any political party influences. Studies and reports from the Centers were sent to the President. Those that received his approval were sent on to Congress so that changes to existing laws could be made where necessary.

With the exception of foreign affairs, the work of the Congress during Henry Quince's terms in office was mostly concerned with the recommendations coming from these Centers. The Center for Election Reform, for example, had come up with a proposal that did away with political party politics, and eliminated elections conducted by physical polls around the nation.

The Center recommended a citizens' compulsory voting system focused on national policy issues. The intention was to replace the presidential popularity contests heretofore in effect. Each citizen over the age of eighteen was to be issued a dedicated laptop-communicating computer that connected him to his federal government by e-mail. The initial expense of these personal computers would be offset by doing away with polling stations, eliminating the inessential ballyhoo of party conventions, political ads, and candidate travel expenditures, and by getting rid of regularly scheduled elections using thousands of state polling stations. Ivan was convinced that the country could save billions of dollars in this way.

The Center for Immigration Reform took over the work that Ivan and his Finders had initiated, and eventually the Finder function became an elite force within the Immigration Department, similar to the special forces of the military departments. It became a sort of peaceful strike force that conducted targeted immigrant recruiting raids, and its Finder Agents succeeded in locating many desirable immigrants. These recruits became leading citizens of the U.S.N.A., which was exactly what Welland intended. Political science finally became scientific. Government turned the spotlight on itself. It was examining, experimenting, and testing its functioning with an eye to efficient, continual improvement. In time, taking the politics out of government made the new nation of North America into the unrivalled leader of human civilization. Those fortunate citizens of Canada and the United States who had had the perspicacity and vision to see the potential of merging their nations became quickly the most prosperous and successful people on the planet.

By the end of President Quince's second five-year term in office, the new nation had attained a universal prosperity that was recognized everywhere. It was impossible to keep this success a secret. The purpose of the State Department had shifted from shepherding the country's major interests to teaching and sharing the methods learned in the quest for peace and prosperity with the international community. Those individuals who had played a part in the success of the new nation necessarily grew older and were presented with other opportunities, and so it was with the original Finders.

Commander Mary O'Neal and Captain John Mercer, after struggling for years to control their attraction to each other in favor of career advancement, finally surrendered to Cupid's will. They were married before the entire Finders complement in the National Cathedral in Washington, D.C. They both served their country until they were eligible for Navy pensions, at which point they bought a horse farm in Virginia and became country squires. They had two boys, who had no shortage of testosterone.

Colonel Craig Cutler also served out his time to earn his pension. He retired as a Brigadier General and went home to Las Vegas, Nevada. His long-suffering wife, Naomi, had weathered many separations over the years of his service. While she waited for her husband to come home from his many far-flung assignments, she decided to make her own career in the hospitality business. When Cutler retired they took a long vacation to Hawaii to discuss their future plans. The Brigadier couldn't bear the thought of being idle, and his wife wasn't ready to give up her job. The compromise they worked out allowed her to keep her job as hotel manager of one of the largest casino-hotels on the strip, and by using her influence she was able to get her husband a job as assistant director of security operations at the hotel.

A year or two later his boss retired and Cutler was put in

charge. His friends claimed that his hotel and casino was the most spit and polish security operation in the nation, and they were right. They had no children and consequently they avoided that ever-popular drain on their expendable income. Using Naomi's contacts in the industry, the couple was able to travel the world. The Colonel, an experienced amateur photographer, compiled an electronic diary of their travels that was consulted by interested bloggers worldwide.

Although Byron Begley and Mike Dickerson had known each other professionally for many years, they developed a close friendship while working as Finders. When they retired from government service they became partners in a private law firm that specialized in immigration and in matters of federal jurisprudence. The experience they had acquired as government lawyers was invaluable to clients on the other side of legal issues, and eventually Begley & Dickerson became a prestigious Washington law firm. Byron continued to mourn the loss of his fiancée, Lily McConnell, and he never married. Lily had been murdered to keep her from testifying in the government's conspiracy case against the Democratic National Committee in the time before the U.S. and Canada merged to form the U.S.N.A. Mike Dickerson and his wife had twins, a boy and a girl. Both were studying in law school and planned to follow in their dad's illustrious footsteps.

Barry Mendelson was selected to be Inspector General of the I.R.S. In this role he was able to apply the knowledge of taxation he had acquired as a special agent and auditor for the Finders, using it to assess the effectiveness of the procedures and staff of the department. The job was demanding, for this was the time when the U.S. Tax Code was blended with the Canadian tax system to create the progressive, simplified flat tax made famous by the U.S.N.A. Barry also became the dedicated father that his wife Brooklyn expected. The fact that his job was located in Washington and required a minimal amount of travel went a long way to keep peace in their family.

For her part Brooklyn, who had been Ivan Welland's assistant during his passage to the lofty government positions in which he had served, was at peace with her position as Ivan's amanuensis and chief factotum. It became understood after a short while that her career was welded to his own in a "Whither thou goest, I shall go" fashion. Brooklyn had had a crush on Ivan from the very first day he had shown up for work at the State Department as an inexperienced academic from Harvard. He was so innocent and likeable that even though he was younger than Brooklyn by a few years, she developed feelings for him that she had kept secret. When Ivan married Marina her clandestine bubble had burst, and she was able to get on with her own personal life.

That was when Barry had come along. Although she continued to be hitched to Ivan's career star, she was well and truly married to her husband. Barry wasn't in the least bit jealous of Ivan. That was one of the things that Brooklyn loved about him, and as it happened, the two men got along famously together. All those who worked with Ivan counted themselves lucky, for he had the true leader's natural talent for encouraging others. Once someone earned Ivan's respect, it was his or hers for life.

CHAPTER THIRTEEN

As far as Ivan Welland was concerned, his career was as exciting as his personal life was miserable. His daughter Julia had graduated from high school with honors, and received her acceptance letter from her father's alma mater. On the same day that Julia received the good news from Harvard University, Marina, Ivan's wife, got the call from her oncologist that everybody dreads: she had contracted pancreatic cancer, and she was already at a very advanced stage of her illness.

Marina and Ivan had been shocked by the news.

"Pancreatic cancer tends to be silent and painless as it grows," her oncologist had informed them. "By the time it's advanced enough to cause symptoms, the cancer has usually grown outside the pancreas, and I'm afraid that's what has happened in your case, Marina."

"I was losing weight, that's all," Marina had said tearfully. "I was glad to be losing weight. I just had a little back pain, but I thought that was because we were doing some redecorating. There were lots of books that had to be put away, and there was furniture to be moved... I only moved it just a little bit, not enough to cause me any physical harm."

"Your cancer was found in the tail of the pancreas," the oncologist had explained. "When it's found in that location it tends to be symptom-free, or essentially symptom-free, so you mustn't blame yourself for not knowing what was going on in your body."

"I had some diarrhea," Marina confessed, "but it never occurred to me to go and see a doctor about a little diarrhea. I thought it was because I was drinking too much coffee. I was feeling a bit tired, you see. That's why I was drinking so much coffee," she added apologetically. "But I was glad to give it up. It tasted horrible. I couldn't find any coffee in D.C. that didn't taste like mud from the bottom of a river."

Sadly for Marina and Ivan what the surgeon had found, and what the pathology laboratory confirmed, constituted the worst possible news. The cancer had already metastasized to some distant lymph nodes in her abdominal cavity. Within a relatively short period of time Ivan had become a widower and Julia was motherless.

The funeral was attended by Ivan's friends, Marina's colleagues and students, and various family members. The bereaved husband and his only child faced the future without enthusiasm. Ivan and Julia knew they had to get on with life, but they had a great deal of difficulty doing it.

Ivan saw to it that Julia got up to Cambridge and into her dormitory room at the start of the fall semester, but he was unhappy and unbearably lonely when he returned to the empty brownstone house in Georgetown where the three of them had lived for so many years. He missed Marina with all his heart, and he felt as if he could never become enthusiastic about anything ever again. Julia's attendance at Harvard, of course, was exciting for her proud father, but it would have been so much more so if only Marina could have been there to share the experience.

It was at the height of his loneliness that Ivan received a call from the White House asking him to come in to see President Henry Quince. When Ivan was seated in the plush armchair in the Oval Office, the President's secretary offered him a cup of coffee or an alcoholic beverage, both of which he politely declined.

After the secretary left the room, Ivan looked at Quince expectantly, curious to hear what he had to say. After all, it was not every day that he was invited to the people's house to have a chat with the chief executive.

"How are you doing these days, Ivan?" the President asked him, hoping to find out how he was getting along without Marina.

"I'm doing the best I can to get over the death of my wife, but I miss her terribly."

President Quince had lost his wife a few years before, also to cancer, so he knew what Ivan was going through, and he sympathized.

"Ivan, I found the best thing to do is work. My advice to you is to go to work on some project that you love and lose yourself in it, and of course I happen to have such a project in mind."

"Why am I not surprised, Henry? But I suppose you're right. I do need to get my teeth into something meaningful so I can stop gnawing on myself. What did you have in mind?"

"Remember when you were heading up that non-profit think tank, Ivan? Remind me, what was it called?"

"The Foundation for Democracy Research, or the FDR. I ran that organization for a few years between government appointments."

"Right. I seem to remember that when you were there, you published a proposal to change the Presidency of the United States from one elected individual to a nine-person ruling executive committee whose members were selected by merit. Am I right?"

"You have a good memory, Henry. However, that was a proposal intended for consideration by the United States, and it pre-dated the formation of the United States of North America."

"I know that, but I'd like you to dust that proposal off and make it suitable for the U.S.N.A. I don't think the U.S. was ready back then for such a new idea, but the U.S.N.A. is a completely different kettle of fish. Keep this between us, all right? I still have several years to go in office."

"I don't quite follow. What has one thing got to do with the other?"

"I'm of the opinion that this idea could only take hold if an incumbent president introduced it."

"An incumbent president? But why, Henry? You know

much more about my proposal than anyone else does. You'd be the best one to introduce it and to follow it up to make sure it didn't have any glitches."

"I have to disagree with you there, Ivan. I know one person who is much better suited to put the idea forward than I would be myself."

"What? Who? How can anyone else know the details of the proposal better than you?"

"Just think for a moment, Ivan. Who do you suppose I'm referring to?"

"I'm afraid I have no idea."

"Come now, Ivan. You can drop the modesty."

"No, Henry, no. You can't mean it."

"Listen to me carefully. The U.S.N.A. was my idea, and I was the one elected to bring the merged nations of Canada and the United States into a North American unity. That's a big job for one man, but fortunately I was able to accomplish the unification."

"Exactly! So why wouldn't you be the perfect one to institute the new changes?"

The President held up his hand to silence Ivan for a moment.

"My job now is to remove or debug all the obstacles in the way of a smoothly running government. My successor could make it his purpose to install certain refinements that would call for constitutional amendments, congressional approval, and nationwide citizen support. We both know that one man can't properly govern an entity like this country. It was your idea to broaden the executive branch and make it more effective, so you should be the one to implement your suggestions. Therefore, I'd like you to be my successor. You must run for the office of President."

"I see," Ivan said, putting his chin in his hand. "That's very flattering, Henry, but I have to think about all the many ramifications of such a step before I can make a decision."

"Naturally, Ivan. Take all the time you need, but bear in

mind that you're one of the few men with enough character to be willing and able to voluntarily share power with others for the sake of a higher good."

"It's kind of you to think so highly of me, but there are myriad difficulties to be overcome before such basic changes in our democracy can be implemented."

"All too true, Ivan, but I propose that we form a Center for Executive Branch Research, which you could head up starting immediately. The Center could do all the preparatory work needed to develop your idea to change the presidency from a single executive chosen by the citizenry in an election based on a mass popularity contest, to a supreme executive body of nine merit-tested persons chosen via a process of universal, compulsory, electronic voting. In this way you could use the work of the Center as the foundation of your platform in the last two-party elections ever held."

"I'm flattered that you liked the proposal that came from the FDR. It's clever of you to see the wisdom of including the idea of a multiple person presidency in your successor's platform. Needless to say, it would be especially advantageous if the heir to your office were to be me. If the Judicial Branch needs nine judges to make up the Supreme Court, and the two-body Legislative Branch of U.S.N.A. has 120 members in the Senate and over 500 people in the House, certainly the Executive Branch should include at least the same number as the judiciary."

"Indeed. Take some time to think about my proposal, Ivan. Then get back to me as soon as you've made your decision. There's no time to waste."

Ivan did as the President asked. He wished he could have talked about it with Marina the way they used to discuss everything when she was alive. As things were, he talked to a few of his trusted friends, and thought about the implications of the President's offer. After a few days he called President Quince with his decision, which was partly a counter-proposal.

"Well Ivan, have you made a decision?"

"I have, Mr. President."

"Well, what will it be?"

"I think I would like to head up the Center for Executive Branch Research, but I wonder if we need to decide about my running for President right away. I mean, you have eight more years in office if you run for reelection. In that time a lot could change. Could we defer the decision on my running for President until we see what the Center comes up with for a recommendation?"

"Sure, we can do it your way, but I want your decision on the run for the presidency as soon as I'm reelected for a second term, presuming I'm given a second term."

So Dr. Ivan Welland became the Director of the Center for Executive Branch Research. Few men, if any, had his extensive experience in the various parts of the Executive Branch. He had held senior positions in the Departments of State, Defense, Justice, and Homeland Security, and he had been a principal researcher in a non-profit think tank, but he had never held an elected office. The idea of running for the highest elected office had been anathema to him until the President had suggested that he could be the *last* individual president. The merit of the idea of an expanded presidency would be enhanced if the present President were willing to surrender sole ownership of the title. Ivan had always been apolitical. His loyalty to his country was far stronger than his allegiance to any political party.

The U.S.N.A. offered the citizens of both countries a perfect opportunity to make some needed changes to the laws of both Canada and the U.S. Ivan seemed to see this opportunity more clearly than anyone else, so perhaps he was indeed the best one to shepherd in the changes that had to be made to the democratic system in order for it to survive into the future. Now that three hundred years had passed since the creation of the original constitution, the population would surely see the wisdom of making a few adjustments to that venerable document in the light of the new challenges brought about by the passage of time and the developments that had occurred in the intervening eras. The founders knew or at least suspected that the document they were writing was imperfect. That is why they provided the new nation with an amending procedure. Can anyone imagine the Constitution without the Bill of Rights?

At the time of the U.S.N.A.'s foundation, the term of the office of President was changed to five years. So when Henry Quince brought up the question of Ivan's candidacy for the presidency, there were four years remaining in his first term, and five more if he got a second term in office. Therefore, Ivan's election, if he were to be elected, was a good way off, and Ivan maintained himself in a temporary state of denial. He hunkered down in his old role as an academic and devoted himself fully to directing the Center for Executive Branch Research, refining the proposals put forward by the Foundation for Democracy Research, the Washington think tank that he had formerly directed.

A widely-read and much-discussed novel was published a year or so after the FDR made its recommendations. It was entitled *The Election of Everyman*, and written by Aidan de Vries. In this book the author described an evolved United States federal government, using the material put out by the FDR. Ivan had liked the book, particularly the concise style that de Vries had used to describe the imagined changes to the U.S. Constitution that were developed in his story. On a whim, Ivan had contacted the author and they hit it off. As a result, he decided to invite de Vries to serve as a consultant writer in preparing the papers that would lead to the drafting of the constitutional amendments. It would be necessary, of course, to turn the fictional plans into legal terminology.

Ivan and Aidan thought of it as a nouveau Jefferson-Madison partnership. The main task of the Center was to design an improved Executive Branch. They intended the

Center to be a mini-constitutional convention without the handicap of strident party politicians. Since the U.S.N.A. was not the U.S., they were not worried about tampering with the venerated American Constitution.

The Center needed a constitutional lawyer who knew how to draft the types of legislation that would allow action to be taken on the Center's recommendations. Ivan contacted Mike Dickerson and persuaded him to come out of retirement to help the Center with this work. Mike and Ivan knew each other well and had a deep level of trust for each other. And, of course, after a lifetime of working together, Ivan could scarcely imagine not having his assistant, Brooklyn, on board. This was the complement of people who would dare to improve on the U.S. Constitution in order to better serve the needs of the United States of North America. The work took over six years to complete. Only Ivan had the slightest idea that this work could take so long, and only he knew that the work of the Center would form the principal planks in the platform of the next candidate for President, which would turn out to be Ivan himself.

President Henry Quince would check periodically to see how the work was advancing. Ivan considered the President to be the *éminence grise* of the project, for without Quince's enthusiastic ratification and his presidential clout, it would not have been possible to institute the idea of a multi-person executive, the dissolution of political parties, and the use of electronic technology as a tool to improve the efficiency of the elections. Quince was also in favor of polling candidates based on issues rather than on popularity. The fact that the suggestion came from a sitting president was enough to get the attention of the Supreme Court and the citizenry too. The public was also intrigued by the powerful novelty of an individual like Ivan Welland running for the presidency and being willing to share the office.

* * * *

Ivan's daughter, Julia, had finished her clerkship in the office of the Justice of the Supreme Court, and now she was being pursued by several large Washington law firms. The starting salaries she was being offered amazed Ivan. He couldn't help wondering how they could extend such generous offers to a person just beginning her career. It was true that she was an obvious talent, but he couldn't help wondering if some of the attention was due to the Welland name. He knew that Julia would be expected to deliver some degree of influence with a father who was being considered for the presidency. Ivan worried that her career might be adversely affected if he lost the election. He also was concerned that because he was alone now, Julia would feel obligated to take a job that kept her near him instead of being free to choose her own future.

In spite of all his excellent intentions, Ivan entered the competition for his daughter's services. Her specialty was constitutional law and his Center was totally immersed in the same subject. Furthermore, if he were elected to the White House, he would need a surrogate First Lady, as he no longer had a wife. It was his hope that his trusted daughter could serve in that capacity. He decided to bring up the idea with her before she settled on another job. Since they were both very busy and neither had much interest in culinary matters, it was their habit to go out to dinner together once a week. It was at one of these dinners that Ivan decided to ask his only child if she would consider working in the family business.

They were a striking couple. The obvious difference in their ages sometimes caused restaurant patrons to smile, as if he were a sugar daddy and she were his paramour. More for fun than anything else, father and daughter played into this role by holding hands to tease the busybodies and give them even more to gossip about. Ivan, at six foot seven, and Julia at six foot two, made a tall target as they engaged in serious conversation in front of the Washington celebrity-watchers.

"Julia," Ivan began, a bit tentatively. "I was wondering if you would ever consider working with your old Dad."

"I thought you'd never ask!" Julia said enthusiastically.

"Well, I wanted you to explore all your options without feeling obligated to do the family thing. That wasn't a bad decision, was it?"

"No, but they say that faint heart never won fair maiden. I was beginning to think you didn't want me, or that you felt I wasn't experienced enough to work with you."

"I just wanted you to explore the job market, that's all. So, have you had sufficient time to evaluate your worth?"

"Yes, but I'd like to hear what you have to offer."

"Well it's not money, that's for sure. The Center is a non-profit organization, so I can't meet the fantastic money offers you've had. Furthermore, if you work with me you'll always be subject to charges of nepotism, and you'll be in my shadow for a while as far as your work is concerned."

"You're not selling the job very well, Dad."

"I know, but I want to be fair. On the other hand if you work with me you'll have an opportunity to do worthwhile things on the highest level. I've kept you informed about what I'm doing at the Center for Executive Branch Research. This work will form the most important part of my campaign platform if I decide to make a run for the presidency. If I'm elected I'll be making changes to the accepted method of doing the government's business. There'll no doubt be fierce opposition from both the left and the right. The people's traditional view of the office of the President will have to change. Since I'm unmarried now, I'll need you to be my surrogate First Lady if I'm elected. All of this is, of course, up to your discretion. So would you like to accompany your Dad on this political adventure?"

"Before I give you my answer I just want to tell you that I'm grateful beyond words for the wonderful upbringing that you and Mom provided. I hope I've never behaved like a spoiled brat, though I suspect I approached that point at times. But I just want you to know that whatever I am and whatever I've achieved up to this moment, I owe to you."

"This is beginning to sound as if you're getting ready to reject my offer."

"No Dad, quite the opposite. How could I ever refuse to help you? I just wanted you to know that I truly admire you for your actual abilities and accomplishments, and not just because you're my father. I'm the one person in the world who truly and honestly knows how great you are and how lucky the people of North America will be to have you as their President. There now, I've said it. When do you want me to start work?"

"You haven't asked me how much I'll pay or what the conditions and benefits are."

"I'll take whatever you offer me, as long as I can live on it independently. I have no conditions, and the benefits of working alongside you will exceed those that any insurance plan can pay me. There, that's settled. Now let's eat."

Julia had evolved into an incipient deputy campaign manager for her father. She could do no more because he hadn't yet announced his candidacy. She wanted her father to be President because she knew he would do a terrific job, but she was less than enthusiastic about putting him through the stress of a political campaign. Since the formation of the U.S.N.A., the travel during the buildup to the election was greater than ever. The U.S.N.A. was now the largest country in the world. From the North Pole to the Florida Keys, the Yukon to Baja California, the land included every sort of contour. The inhabitants were the most diversified of any nation. From the Inuits in the North, the Latinos in the South, and the immigrants from everywhere on earth, the citizens of the U.S.N.A. were entitled to one vote per person, and candidates for national office hoped to reach them all. The one thing that drove Julia to encourage her dad to run for election was the knowledge that if he won, it would be the last such election. Future candidates would no longer have to drive themselves to the brink of total fatigue. The drain on the candidates, on the nation's coffers, and the cost of proliferating party-inspired lies and half-truths would cease in the future if her dad were elected.

Welland's most original platform plank recommended an almost totally amended electoral system. It used the incredible capabilities of the computer to assure the future of democracy. The system was fair, efficient, tamper-proof, and would save the taxpayers billions of dollars every time there was an election. Ivan and David Feingold had worked out the main part of their improved computerized electoral system. When Julia studied their plan she wondered why it couldn't be combined with the Internal Revenue Service's taxpayer filing system. When her father heard Julia's suggestion he discussed it with David, who thought it had great potential. Welland put David and Julia to work immediately to develop the first-ever interactive simultaneous government and citizen's tax and voting computer application.

If statisticians could tell sportscasters the pitching or batting history of every player in the major leagues in real time, then the same thing could be done for citizens trying to evaluate the voting records of people running for office. When voting was tied to taxation, the need for a simplified income tax system became self-evident. That was the second plank in Ivan Welland's platform. The disbanding of political parties was an obvious result of an election system where citizens voted from home on their own computers, and this became the third plank in Ivan's platform.

The Center for Executive Branch Research evolved naturally into a hotbed of discourse. Welland's platform was refined and the constitutional impediments were identified and marked for amendment. No new idea was rejected out of hand—every idea was argued back and forth until it was included, amended, or excluded. One example was the discussion of how an unqualified or unproductive person could become a member of the nine-person Executive Branch that the Center was considering as the replacement for the office of President.

"Ivan, isn't it undemocratic to prohibit certain people from voting?" Brooklyn asked him one day.

"If you're referring to the qualifying test provision, why shouldn't we have a civics test for voters? We have to take written tests before we can get a driver's license. We don't allow just anyone to get behind the wheel of a car."

"Yes, but democracy means government by the consent of the governed. If you prohibit someone from voting you'll be taking away the basic right of consent."

"Voting is a responsibility, or it should be. We already have restrictions on the right to vote, such as age, citizenship, and residence requirements, so why not require citizens to pass a civics test before being allowed to vote?"

"All schools teach civics, so a test is redundant."

"Students who pass the civics course could be certified and exempted from the test, but what about landed immigrants? We can't know if they've taken a civics class. We have a new country now and Canadians that have become part of the U.S.N.A. didn't study U.S. civics either."

"True, but we're shooting for inclusion, not exclusion."

"Yes, Brooklyn, but we have the example of the Romans to learn from. They had a Senate and laws, but when they tried to include the Barbarians, the Empire went to hell."

"That's ancient history, Ivan. Things are different now. We have laws and we claim that ignorance of the law is no excuse. People learn from experience."

"Ignorance may be no excuse, but it's an explanation. Masses of ignorant people can outvote the educated citizens, and this could ultimately lead to the decline and fall of our brand new country, just as their inclusion as citizens did during the Roman Empire."

"But we still owe our citizens the right to vote, Ivan."

"No, Brooklyn, the right to vote is a privilege, not a right, and every privilege comes with responsibility. The prime responsibility of voting citizens is that they be educated so that their votes have merit. Furthermore, the citizens will never be properly educated until we have overthrown the two-party system with its inevitable schisms. We have an example of the divisiveness of the two-party system that came to a head in the time of President Obama in the United States and made the country dysfunctional. The two parties couldn't even create a budget. Those who ignore the study of the Romans will miss the pointed analogy of the comparison of the American red and blue parties with those of the green and blue parties who slaughtered each other during the reign of the Emperor Justinian."

"Ivan, you're an elitist!"

"You may say that, but I don't want to prevent anyone from voting. I just want voters to have the benefit of an education that enables them to think rationally about the policies and laws that are being voted upon. I don't believe in the manifesto that claims that every vote counts. I believe voting is a serious business, and only serious votes should count. Ten times nothing is nothing. You get what you pay for, not what you deserve. I don't subscribe to the blind patriotism that says 'My country, right or wrong.' It's that kind of thinking that turned our elections into popularity contests in which voting decisions were based on such irrelevant things as appearance, or pigmentation, or party affiliation. Many elections have been decided by opportunistic individuals who were callously pursuing their own ends, without regard to the national good."

Arguments and discussions such as this one raged on for years at the Center for Executive Branch Research. In the end they produced a document that, although it didn't totally satisfy everybody, did at least cover the basics well enough so that all the Fellows at the Center could sign on to it, and Ivan could use it as his platform.

CHAPTER FOURTEEN

P resident Quince nominated Ivan Welland for President of the U.S.N.A. After a short period of time his party decided to make his nomination unanimous. Welland guessed that the debates leading up to previous nominating conventions had absorbed so much energy and expenditures that barring the arrival of the Messiah, the party preferred to just pick someone rather than throw open the doors of the White House to one and all.

By letting his name stand, the election campaign became Welland's world for the next few months. None of this was surprising, as no other candidate could possibly have had better qualifications for the job than Dr. Ivan Welland. As for Welland himself, he could understand how he might be considered the right man for the job, but he believed that the job was too big for any one man. He convinced himself that he could ram his changes through Congress before his first term ended, and that the presidency would become, like the Supreme Court, a nine-person office following the recommendations of the Center for Executive Branch Research before he would be expected to seek reelection.

Many presidents of the nations of the earth have come and gone, but the number of truly humble men and women who have held this office can be counted on the fingers of one hand. Ivan Welland, if he had to be a leader, wanted to be one of these humble ones who, without pomp, overrode circumstance. Having been a Christian all his life without firm denominational attachments, he was nevertheless able to empathize with Jesus of Nazareth when it came to his humility, which was so monumentally powerful that the world has never forgotten it. Ivan felt sure that men had historically

earned the right to be humble, because their unfailingly egotistical acts had certainly proved futile. Ivan hated the idea
that he might be thought to be on a power trip in seeking the
highest office in the land.

The nominating convention went exactly as planned by
President Henry Quince and supporters of Ivan Welland's
candidacy. Quince made the nominating speech on Ivan's
behalf. In it he reminded the delegates of the difficult years
in the past when finding a competent president was a matter
of choosing the man who would be the most appealing to the
electorate. The voters' selections back then, he explained,
were generally made on the basis of personal choice. The
nation's interests were secondary to the individual citizen's
judgment of the candidate's attractiveness and the voter's
expectations of personal gain.

"It's no wonder," Quince said, "that we got presidents of
surprisingly mediocre talent when people lined themselves
up with the party or the candidate who promised to benefit
their personal economic aspirations the most. Yet we have
always known that the electoral system should reflect competency in leadership, not popularity, vain fiscal promises, or
unrealistic visions of the world's future. It's not a valid question for a voter to ask which untested candidate's policies
would be most likely to put money in his pocket. Instead, we
should be asking ourselves what is the best way to ensure
that our nation moves forward in a peaceful way, and which
candidate is most likely to bring about that result."

The President went on to say that he now knew from
personal experience that one man could not truly do justice
to the enormous job of the presidency. Then he led into the
explanation of how one man could, however, suggest ways
to get around the problem by sharing the job, not with just
anybody, but with a few tested and selected candidates of
superior merit. He then publicly nominated Dr. Ivan Welland
as President of the U.S.N.A. because he was, as President

Henry Quince had already suggested, the one man who could successfully change the previous rules of the game. When it was Ivan's turn to speak he arose from his seat and thanked the President for nominating him. Then, after accepting the nomination, he laid out his plan whereby the Executive Branch would be reorganized and the electoral system updated using modern technology to effect various changes that would put the vast country of the U.S.N.A. into a new age of efficiency. It would be a period when leaders earned the right to lead, and citizens were required to register their votes on serious issues. He told the delegates that all it would take at the first stage of an election was to select an individual who would follow the recommendations of the Center for Executive Branch Research. That person would have to be willing to forego the crown, so to speak. He or she would oversee the transition process, and turn the office into a wiser form of governing. He ended his acceptance speech by assuring the audience that he would do everything in his power to be the right man for the job.

The minute Ivan Welland became an official candidate, enemies appeared from everywhere like cockroaches coming out of the woodwork. These were not only the opposing candidate and his minions, but a particularly venomous media that feared that their political influence would be curtailed by Ivan Welland's direct voter program. If his system became established, billions of dollars in advertising revenue would become superfluous. Mandatory electronic voting would do away with the vaunted ground games of the political parties. The nonsense surrounding previous American and Canadian elections would be ended. Citizens would no longer even know the name of the head civil servant any more than they knew the name of the person that reviews their tax return. An anonymous presidency would remove all the egotistical motivations for gaining political office. Executive power would shift from an individual to the anonymous group of nine, and decisions would be rendered consensually.

Since the new system appeared initially to be somewhat complex, the Center for Executive Branch Research prepared a booklet that explained in detail all aspects of the proposed U.S.N.A. federal election system. Ivan Welland, permitting himself to display some pride of authorship, considered the booklet to be a masterpiece of clarity and its implementation the future for democratic voting. The citizenry for whose benefit the publication had been created was, of course, highly averse to change. Welland, brilliant man that he was, had underestimated the ability of the average voter to think creatively for the long term. He had also neglected to take into account the voters' reticence to make real changes in the government of the new nation, regardless of how good they might be.

One of Welland's favorite themes was the inability of the masses to appreciate wisdom in political policy. Numbers simply didn't equate with the ability to generate quality ideas. Ivan's booklet explained that every large progressive step for governing mankind had first to be conceived of and presented by an individual thinker/philosopher/ruler.

"Most of the governing systems of the world," he went on to explain during his acceptance speech for his candidacy to the presidency of the U.S.N.A., "are systems that have undergone vast changes through the centuries, changes that generally came about as a result of violence. Occasionally elections did bring about systemic changes, but they were often changes that were not for the better."

Welland wanted his suggested changes to be peaceful and clearly beneficial to the maturing nation of the U.S.N.A. It would be of benefit to everyone if these changes were to provide a good example of a continually improving modern democracy. Theories and practices of governing, often more inspired by Attila the Hun than the Age of Technology, were still altogether too common, and Welland wanted to prove that there were better ways for civilization to prosper than those used by the political brigands of the world.

Dr. Welland carried his message to the campaign trail. He went to towns and cities complimenting the citizens for having brought about the merger of two countries in a peaceful fashion, and telling them it was now time for them to continue their initiative by installing a new election system. He delivered speeches on television, and learned to present his suggestions in a clear and cogent fashion.

Hundreds of times he went carefully over the plan that he and the Center had designed. He saw to it that a copy of the booklet describing the Center's recommendations was given to everyone who attended his speeches and rallies. At the end of every speech he closed with a summary of how much money would be saved by using home computers for electing leaders. He always included the cost of maintaining political parties, never forgetting to mention the divisive effect they had on the governance of the nation. He conducted a campaign that was honest, thoughtful, and forward-looking, but was this the stuff that gets a man elected?

Welland's opponent was an old-line political hack that had been around Washington politics since before the merger of Canada and the U.S., which incidentally he voted against when he was in the U.S. Senate. Hoping that his position on the merger had been forgotten, he now was running for the job of chief executive of the U.S.N.A. As if this were not ironic enough, his platform consisted mainly of clichés about traditional values. Even Welland, who had a reasonably good imagination, could not see how his opponent could possibly win by using such an uninspired campaign theme.

He had not reckoned with the inability of voters to focus on the important things, and their exasperating propensity to to be captivated by selfish or superficial interests.

WHEN THE STATE DEPARTMENT sends Harvard PhD student Ivan Welland to Chechnya, he sees it as a perfect chance to gather material for his dissertation. Little does he know that he will soon become involved with an imam in a local mosque who turns out to be one of the most dangerous Islamic jihadist terrorists in the Muslim world. Thus begins an exciting and challenging mission in the life of this bookish academic. He discovers the headquarters of a council of caliphs that directs terrorist attacks worldwide, and he uses his academic training to come up with a startling plan for mounting a successful counterterrorist attack on jihadists everywhere, while at the same time avoiding the tragedy of collateral damage.

This is the second edition of the popular novel by Aidan de Vries. *Finders* now completes the seven volumes featuring Dr. Ivan Welland and his famous team of problem solvers.

Available on Amazon and on erserandpond.com

WHEN CAPTAIN NIKO CONSTANTINE (able seaman and womanizer of note) is selected to command the largest cruise ship in the world, he looks forward to enjoying the most challenging, exciting journey of his life. But what he doesn't know is that a group of jihadist terrorists is plotting to turn the luxury liner's maiden voyage into a trip to hell.

Once again Aidan de Vries has written a riveting story about Ivan Welland, the hero of *Council of Caliphs,* who is suddenly called upon to save the carefree passengers from certain death. This time, right out of the blue, he and his team of brave collaborators are given some assistance from an unprecedented quarter.

AIDAN DE VRIES was born in New York. He worked for a time with the FBI, and later started a business of his own as an executive recruiter. This is his second novel.

Available on Amazon and on erserandpond.com

The Peacemaker
Aidan de Vries

AFTER A METEORIC RISE in the government, Harvard PhD Ivan Welland us appointed Secretary of Defense by the newly-elected President. By understanding that defense is not possible until peace is secured, he evolves a plan whereby, with the help of his faithful team and some remarkable supporters, he is able to thwart the many enemies of global harmony and offer the President a brilliant new program to make peace and true defense a welcome reality for all.

This is the third thriller in the series about Dr. Ivan Welland's adventurous life as he and his team dedicate themselves to returning the U.S.A. to the original principles of the Founding Fathers.

Available on Amazon and on erserandpond.com

WHEN IVAN WELLAND DISCOVERS that the freedom of the press provision of the Bill of Rights is about to be exploited by an international media conglomerate, he is forced to come to terms with what may be some basic flaws in our democratic system. His investigative team delves into the world of international mergers and acquisitions, and discovers that the people in control of words and graphics can be at least as worrisome to the Department of Defense as terrorists armed with guns and bombs. Is the media obligated to report the truth, or does the First Amendment protect a reporter's right to twist the facts? Is America only a reflection of the hidden agendas of various interested parties?

In this fourth political thriller by Aidan de Vries, hero Ivan Welland is cast into a dangerous void where appearance and reality become blurred. The reader is challenged, along with Dr. Welland, to re-examine the meaning and perception of truth, and how it should be presented to the public.

Available on Amazon and on erserandpond.com

WHEN THE NEW PRESIDENT TAKES OFFICE, Dr. Ivan Welland's term as Secretary of Defense is over. He agrees to chair the Foundation for Democracy Research, with a mandate to design a presidential election system that will better serve America. Welland soon learns about secret machinations that take place without the knowledge of the voters, and that have huge consequences for Americans. His efforts to restore democracy, amend the Constitution, and force the corrupt and treasonous President to return to the principles of the founding fathers becomes a deadly adventure that takes the reader into the realm of murderous power mongers, FBI investigations, and federal prosecutions by the U.S. Attorney General. This thought-provoking cautionary tale is the fifth political thriller by Aidan de Vries. It may be prescient in its reflection of possible future events, and is sure to challenge every reader's idea of what democracy should be.

Available on Amazon and on erserandpond.com

IN RESPONSE TO THE ECONOMIC CRISIS in the United States, Dr. Ivan Welland decides to take on the challenge of curing the ills that have caused the problems. He leads his non-profit Foundation for Democracy Research into a study of the alphabet soup of regulatory agencies responsible for the economy. We learn about the functions and failings of the SEC, Fed, FDIC, IRS, BIS, OMB, and the network of complexities under which our economy barely survives.

Along the way we discover a plot to defraud the United States Treasury of TARP funds intended to save a bank from insolvency. The reader is led into the center of a corruption scheme which, if successful, would turn out to be the largest known embezzlement in history.

This is the sixth cautionary thriller by Aidan de Vries. It takes us where we need to go to understand the risks that threaten the economic pillars of our democratic system.

Available on Amazon and on erserandpond.com